# THE GUARDIAN:
## DERAILERS

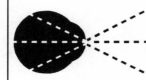

This Large Print Book carries the
Seal of Approval of N.A.V.H.

# THE GUARDIAN: DERAILERS

## TOBIAS COLE

**THORNDIKE PRESS**
A part of Gale, a Cengage Company

A Cengage Company

Farmington Hills, Mich • San Francisco • New York • Waterville, Maine
Meriden, Conn • Mason, Ohio • Chicago

Copyright © 2006 by Cameron Judd.
The Guardian #1.
Thorndike Press, a part of Gale, a Cengage Company.

Thorndike Press® Large Print Western.
The text of this Large Print edition is unabridged.
Other aspects of the book may vary from the original edition.
Set in 16 pt. Plantin.

LIBRARY OF CONGRESS CIP DATA ON FILE.
CATALOGUING IN PUBLICATION FOR THIS BOOK
IS AVAILABLE FROM THE LIBRARY OF CONGRESS

ISBN-13: 978-1-4328-7074-4 (hardcover alk. paper)

Published in 2019 by arrangement with William Morrow, an imprint of HarperCollins Publishers

Printed in Mexico
1 2 3 4 5 6 7 23 22 21 20 19

To Rhoda

# PROLOGUE

The first man crawled out on the ledge and settled himself in hope of a clear view. His movement caused loose gravel to spill over the edge and rattle down the sheer canyon wall into the darkness below. But there was no danger that the gravel would cause him and his nearby companion to be discovered. It was quite dark, the moon intermittently covered by fast-scudding clouds, and the canyon so reverberated with the noise of the speeding train below that the falling gravel would be heard and noticed by no one. And any below already knew the presence of the men above, and were where they were in order to act upon their behalf.

The second man crawled out beside the first and watched the black, smoking iron serpent crawl along the track below. "There it comes."

"Yep." The first man paused, tugging at a cloth that covered his face like a mask, tied in place with a cord across his forehead and another more loosely around his neck, just below chin level. His eyes peered through holes cut in the cloth. "God, I hope this all goes good."

"Are the boys all ready down there?"

"Yep." The masked man pulled a spyglass from his coat pocket, positioned it over the right eyehole in his face cloth, and focused in on the train in the canyon. "Short train, ain't it!"

"I noticed that." The speaker reached up and wiped some grit off his brow, his hand brushing over a distinctive, dark birthmark that spread out in front of his ear like a painted-on sideburn.

"That's how we know for certain that this is the right one," said the other. "Ferrell is too high-and-mighty for anything but his own train, you know. Got to have something special. See that railroad car there in the middle? Fancy-looking house coach . . . they say it's like a little palace inside there. Since Ferrell's gone from being a sorry murdering blue-belly to a rich banker, I guess he figures he's got to be treated like a king." The man lifted the bottom portion of the cloth covering his face and spat in the direction of the train. "This is one killing job I might even have did if nobody was paying

8

for it! I hate Ferrell! Hate his kind!"

"Why's his woman want him killed?"

"The usual reason. Unfaithful to her. Left his wife alone at home while he dallied with a mistress."

"Oh."

"Believe me, Leonard, I understand how that woman feels. How being misused that way makes you burn down inside. My own 'Phelia was unfaithful to me, Leonard. At least, I believe she was. Have I told you that before?"

"Uh . . . you have. Yes."

"I ain't ever forgave her for that, even after all she's been through. I ain't got it in me to forgive. That's one difference between me and Jesus, I guess. You reckon?"

"One of many, Morgan. One of many."

"You know my motto, Leonard."

"Yep."

"Betrayal brings death. But I confess I've never found it in myself to apply that rule to 'Phelia, as bad as she betrayed me. But nature's had its own revenge against her. Not much of a life she's living now laid up in that bed over in St. Louis."

The men held silent a few moments, watching the train progress. It would be nearly out of the canyon in less than a minute. From that moment on, timing had to be perfect. The man in the cloth mask began to wish he'd not put so much of this task into the hands of underlings. They were capable men, and loyal, but the mission was not as personal for them as it was for him. They might be careless, wait a few moments too long, or jump the gun and move too soon.

At the end of the canyon was a wide, deep gully, running right across the canyon mouth and crossed by a small, sturdy bridge. The two watching men reflexively held their breath as the train rumbled closer to the bridge. It all came down to that, the next few moments.

"All right," the first man, Morgan Kirk, whispered, sending out instructions into the night to men who were much too far away to hear him. "Let it blow . . . *now!*"

The two watchers tensed, waiting . . . and nothing happened. The masked one came to his feet and stood on the very edge of the ledge, heedless of the danger, leaning out a little as if he might leap toward the train hurtling along far below him. "Now!" he said, urgently, speaking to his unseen, unhearing men below. Still nothing happened. "Damn it . . . do it *now!*" he screamed. His voice was lost in the rumble of the train and the great emptiness between the canyon walls.

"Watch out, Morgan! You'll fall!" the second man said, now also on his feet. He grasped his partner by the back of his gun-belt, pulling him backward and away from the rim of the canyon.

A rending, brilliant blast shook the canyon and filled the night with light and noise. The little bridge spanning a gully over which the locomotive was passing at that moment shattered to splinters. The locomotive bucked up from the force of the explosion, pitched to one side and twisted down to the base of the gully. The rest of the short train followed. The elaborate private car that had drawn the masked man's scorn pitched over and ruptured like a dropped egg, its expensive woods splintered and contents of the car — wooden, metal, crystalline, fabric, and human — dumped out beside the tracks.

Watching from above, the first man sank to his haunches, stunned. He reached up and jerked the cloth mask off his face. "They waited too long!" he declared. "They were supposed to blow the tracks so the train would derail . . . not blow up the train itself! They should have blown it *before* the train reached the bridge!"

11

The second man watched his companion with an odd expression. "I know . . . but it's all the same result," he said. "Ferrell's bound to be dead now. Nobody could have lived through that."

But then it became evident that someone had. From the bowels of the shattered private car below, a figure moved and staggered away from the wreckage. He would have been invisible to the watchers high above if not for the light of flames that were beginning to lick through the wreckage. Through the veil of thickening smoke, the two men above the canyon watched the obviously injured man put distance between himself and the derailed train.

The man who had worn the mask looked through his spyglass and watched the progress of the escapee from the train. As fire spread through the train, light grew within the canyon and illuminated the faces of the two watchers peering down from the ledge. The second watcher on the ledge felt his eyes drawn to the unmasked face of the first man. As always on those rare times he saw that face uncovered, his heart jumped to his throat as he saw the mercilessly ugly scars and pits that ruined a countenance considered at one time handsome. The second man stared despite himself, though part of him reflexively wanted to turn away and not see the terrible scars.

The scarred man jerked the spyglass away from his eye. "It's *him*!" he said. "He's gotten out alive! *Alive,* damn him!"

The second man flopped onto his belly and crawled to the very edge of the canyon so that his head hung over. "Are you *sure* that's him?"

"It's him, Leonard. The son of a bitch is going to get away from this alive . . . I've derailed a whole damned train just to kill him, and he's going to walk away!"

"Not far, Morgan. He won't walk far. See?"

Two horsemen, associates of the watchers on the ledge, were riding down toward the man stumbling away from the train. The man stopped as they approached, and seemed to be confused. He spoke to them, though the men watching from above could not hear what he said. He waved back toward the derailed train, as if the two riders wouldn't have noticed it without him pointing it out.

One of the mounted men drew a long pistol and leveled it at the man on foot. The latter dropped to his knees and lifted up his hands pleadingly.

"Right pitiful, ain't he?" said Leonard,

watching from the canyon ledge.

The formerly masked one, Morgan, made a disdainful noise, stood tall, and waved at the horsemen below. The one with the pistol looked up at him and motioned toward the kneeling man.

"I think Menko wants to know whether to do it or not," Leonard said to Morgan.

"I can see that, Leonard," replied Morgan. He lifted his right hand, finger pointed like a pistol, then snapped his thumb down and gave the hand a shake as if it were being jolted by pistol recoil. Then he leaned over the edge of the canyon, cupped hands to his mouth, and shouted, "Ferrell!"

The kneeling man, whose very posture and manner spoke of abject terror, looked up. Morgan shouted, speaking slowly and clearly. "Your woman wants you dead, Ferrell! She paid for the job!"

Ferrell looked up at his tormentor on the ledge. As he did so, the man with the pistol, a Morgan Kirk underling named Ben Menko, leveled the weapon and aimed it at the side of Ferrell's head.

The sound of the shot echoed through the canyon, rebounding between the walls. Morgan watched Ferrell pitch over to the side and lie still.

"It's done," Morgan said. "The job's done."

"Where now, Morgan?" Leonard asked.

"Missouri," he said.

"Ah, yeah. Going to see your mother because she's ailing."

"That's part of it, yeah. But not all of it. Remember that wire I got three days ago? Well, it was from Wesley Blue. He says word is out on the pipeline that there's a killing job out for offer right now. Something out of St. Louis, but involving Gullytown, too. I don't know no details yet, but I'll check into it once we hit Missouri."

"Morgan, we should take a look at the Gullytown railroad, see if there might be some decent express shipments coming up. We could do a little train robbing there."

"Depends on whether there would be enough return for the effort. Not a lot of money in Gullytown. Besides, I'm hearing through the mill that the Gullytown line has added some special security. Some sort of special guard."

"Yes, that's true . . . and you know who that guard is?"

"Can't say I do."

"You remember the young fellow, Tennessee boy, who rode with Jim Parsons during the war? Name of Curry, if I recollect rightly."

"I remember him, Leonard. Dylan Curry, I think. Just a young fellow. Didn't stick with Parsons when the war was over. Turned lawman in St. Louis, didn't he?"

"Private detective, to start with. Now he's working for the Gullytown line, guarding the railroad from sorry old bandits like us. And when he ain't on the train he works for the Gullytown marshal as a town deputy. He's getting some fame for that Guardian work he does. There's a story out that he got shot up a while back during a train robbery and still brought down the whole gang of them doing it. It was all wrote up by some reporter and printed all across the nation."

"I don't think he could stop *us,* Leonard. Others, maybe. Not us."

"So maybe you'd consider robbing the Gullytown line after all? I think it would be a fine thing to show that you can't stop the Morgan Kirk gang just by posting yourself some little guard on a railroad line."

"We'll think about it, Leonard. Right now I just want to put this job here behind us, and get up to Missouri to see my old mother in Gryner Hill while she's still alive to be seen."

"Yeah. Yeah." Leonard shut up for a while, studying the wreckage below. He gestured down toward it. "Seems a shame it had to be done that way."

"Don't get soft-hearted on us, Leonard," said Morgan Kirk. "It don't pay in this line of work to be soft-hearted. 'Specially toward such rubbish as Ferrell was. Betrayal brings death. Always remember that. Now let's get the men back together and get out of here before the law shows up."

# 1

Fortune has been good to me in many ways throughout life, giving me a fine family in boyhood, a hardworking father and mother with wisdom beyond their limited schooling, and youthful years that included plenty of time spent roaming fields and forests and stringing trotlines across fish-rich streams. But in one area — women — I'd never had extraordinary luck, mostly because the circumstances of my young manhood had precluded much opportunity for courting.

Add to that that I was a reticent fellow when a boy. Growing up, I was evermore quiet and shy by nature, too much so to pursue the ladies with the vigor I should have. And though I was told more than once that I was a decent-looking figure of a fellow, my quietness had tended to keep some distance between me and the female world at large.

I tell all that to make it clear why it is

noteworthy that, at the point I enter this narrative, I was in the company of the most beautiful woman in all Missouri. And it was by her own choosing she was with me, for it was she who had sat down across from me in the passenger compartment of this train on the Gullytown line, and she who had pursued conversation. She'd introduced herself as "Miss Seabury." The odd thing about it was that she had upon her knee a pad of paper and in her hand a pencil, and seemed intent on writing down everything I said to her. I had no idea why.

She scribbled so intently that she'd already broken the lead from two pencils and was working hard on a third. Her tablet was propped on her leg at an angle that kept me from seeing the words. She gave the pencil a great flourishing sweep, as if underlining something, and broke that third lead, muttering something that might have been a curse, but was too softly spoken to truly hear.

"Are you always so hard on pencils, Miss Seabury?" I asked.

She turned her beautiful face to me and laughed softly. "Oh, it's just bad penmanship, I suppose. I bear down too hard on the lead. I used to break chalk against my slate when I was in school, so I guess it has been a lifelong habit."

"Where was school for you, Miss Seabury? Where did you grow up?"

"Oh, uh . . . Delaware. Have you ever been there?"

"Never been to Delaware, no."

She looked relieved, oddly. "It's small enough that even if you aim to go there, you might miss it," she said.

She leaned over and from the crumpled bag at her feet produced a fourth pencil. She evaluated the sharpened end and wrote again,

I had to ask. "Why are you writing? I feel as if I'm being interviewed."

She laid the pencil and pad to the side for the moment, and turned a frank gaze upon me. "I owe you an explanation. My note-taking habit is one I've been taught to develop. 'A good journalist lives by his . . . or her . . . notepad.' That's what my mentor and teacher tells me. You never know when you might need to remember something you've been told, he says."

"So you're a journalist?"

"Yes . . . well, sort of. I've had a small amount of work published . . . but I guess the real truth is I'm still a journalist in training."

"By this 'mentor' you mentioned."

21

She wrote something else down, frowned at it, then looked up and nodded. "Yes. His name is J.P. Brannigan. He lives in St. Louis, but travels widely. He is one of the most noted writers for the *Monthly American Review.* Are you familiar with that magazine?"

Of course I was. A story about a particular railroad exploit of mine had graced the *Review*'s pages in a recent edition and brought me the closest thing to fame I'd ever experienced . . . though fame wasn't something I'd been looking for, and the story had appeared without my advance knowledge it was coming. "I've seen the *Review.* In fact, there's a boy reading a copy of one now, sitting over in that direction. And I've seen the Brannigan name in it, I think."

"So you do read. You are able."

*Ouch.* "Do I look illiterate?"

"I wasn't trying to imply you 'look' one way or another. One can't tell such things by appearances. It's a simple fact that many people cannot read."

"I'm not one of them. I've been able to read since I attended old Grover Academy back in White County, Tennessee."

"I think I might have offended you, Mr. . . . ." She paused, embarrassed by a memory lapse, and flipped back quickly through her pages of scribbled notes. "Mr. Curry," she said. "Yes. Mr. Dylan Curry. A good name. A strong name." She looked up and smiled at me in flattering fashion, trying hard to cover any offense caused by forgetting my name, but the smile soon trembled away and the look of embarrassment returned. "I'm sorry," she said. "I'm too forgetful sometimes. I don't know why. I should not have forgotten your name."

"Think nothing of it. I do the same thing all the time. Anyway, you just proved the value of your note-taking habit. And by the way, I'd be honored if you'd drop the 'Mister' and simply call me Dylan."

"Dylan Curry," she said, nodding. "I like the ring of that."

She was a big one on names, obviously. "And you, I know, are Miss Seabury. Your first name, though"

"Amanda."

"Amanda Seabury. A lot of poetry there. See? I *am* literate! I even know what poetry is." I grinned broadly at her and she grinned back. Lord, she was beautiful! The very personification of the word. I'd never seen such a face, such a smile.

She laughed. "You are funny, Dylan. I mean that in a good way. You amuse me."

"Well, I can't imagine a higher calling in

life than amusing you, Miss Seabury."

My words had a stronger edge of sarcasm than I had intended. She looked stung, pulled away from me a little and wrote some more on her notepad.

I looked out the window and noticed that we were passing the humble homestead of Paul and Rhoda Aaron, an old couple who had lived in the vicinity longer than most, but who now were too old for either ranching or farming. These days the elderly couple spent most of their time sitting on their porch, as they were now, with Paul whittling walking sticks and Rhoda knitting shawls. There was hardly a woman in Gullytown, which was some miles up the railway, who did not own and cherish one of Rhoda's famous shawls.

Paul's flashing whittling blade and Rhoda's clicking copper knitting needles were soon out of sight as the train sped by. I returned my attention to Amanda Seabury.

"What are you going to do with all those notes?" I asked. "I can't believe I'm worth writing about in the *American Monthly Review* this soon after the earlier story. That story embarrassed me some . . . it had me as some sort of Crockett-like hero, single-handedly holding off an entire gang of train robbers and surviving a hail of bullets at the same time."

"Was that not accurate?" she asked.

"Well, I never thought of myself as a hero."

"But you did hold off the gang of robbers. You did survive a hail of bullets."

She had me there. "Yes."

"Was it true that the confrontation ended with you atop the train, shooting it out with the last of the robbers?"

"It's true."

"Then like it or not, Mr. Dylan Curry, you are indeed a hero. And you are of journalistic interest."

"But surely not so soon after the first story."

"You mustn't assume that what I wish to write is exactly the same kind of story that was written before. Nor even that you would be the subject of the story. It may be, though, that you know some things, and some people, who would be worth writing about. In fact, it is my conviction that you could lead me to certain people that led me to come here and ride this train. People who would definitely be interesting to write about. I've been looking for you, Mr. Guardian. You are the reason I am riding the Gullytown line."

"I'm . . . astonished," I said. "I would have never expected it. But who do you think I can lead you to? Just what kind of stories do you want to write?"

"Have you ever read travel stories? Readers in the East never tire of them. Especially stories of journeys in the West. They sit pasty-faced in their parlors in Boston and New York, clutching their magazines, and read about encounters with Indians and stagecoach rides up mountain roads and try to imagine what it would feel like, and even smell like, to take part in a buffalo hunt."

"You obviously hold that in contempt," I said.

"Why do you think I would have contempt for stagecoach rides or Indian encounters?"

"No, you seem to hold contempt for the idea of people sitting in their parlors and reading about such things."

She shrugged. "I don't think that's true. After all, they are the ones who provide a market for the work of journalists like me . . . or like I hope to be one day. No, what I hold in contempt, I guess, is the habit itself, not the people who have it."

Odd distinction. I didn't follow her. "The habit?" I queried.

"Yes. Of living life in safe little parlors, having adventures through the lives and words of others, instead of getting out of the parlor and out into the world. Why be content to read about riding up a mountain on a stagecoach, or taking aim at a buffalo, or riding on a train with a man who used to help rob them, when you can do it yourself?"

"What did you just say? Something about riding on a train with someone who used to rob them. Amanda, do you believe for some reason that I'm a man who used to rob trains."

She cocked her head. "Well . . . are you?"

I drew in a slow breath, debating what to say to her. In most situations I made no secret of who I was and what I'd done in the past, but in this case I'd have felt much better about openness if I knew more about Amanda Seabury and her intentions for all those notes she was taking. Here was a young woman, traveling alone, talking freely to a stranger and taking abundant notes while claiming herself to be a journalist in training . . . the whole thing put me into an attitude of caution.

The train began to feel close and stuffy; sweat trickled down the back of my neck. It had been cool for days, but now the weather was taking a turn the other way. I wore a light jacket, but for a reason unrelated to the weather. The jacket hid a pistol — I was hesitant at the moment to remove the jacket and reveal the weapon on a crowded train. The pistol would either draw a barrage of new questions from Amanda Seabury or scare her. I decided to leave the coat on for now.

A trickle of sweat down my forehead changed my mind. I slipped off the coat and rolled up my shirtsleeves. I'd also have opened the window but for the fact that Amanda had closed it earlier because of smoke and cinders blowing in from the locomotive smokestack.

When I looked up at Amanda again her gaze was shifting back and forth between the shoulder-harness pistol rig I wore, carrying my small Colt pistol, and a particularly visible and rather ugly pair of scars on my left forearm that I'd exposed by rolling up my sleeve.

"Are you all right, Miss Seabury . . . Amanda?" I asked.

Before she had a chance to answer, old Otto Bracken came shuffling up the aisle, stopping by to chat with passengers in his usual friendly way. Otto punched tickets for the Gullytown line and treated passengers as his personal charges, friendly with all except those whose behavior damaged the hospitable image of the railroad. But Otto often seemed unaware that he had a tendency to intrude into conversations and privacy. It was so obviously well intentioned and unconsciously done, though, that few minded.

"Dylan," Otto said in his hoarse, old-man croak. "I need to have a word with you."

"I'm listening."

Otto glanced at Amanda, a quick flick of the eyes. Eye, actually. His right eye had been lost years before, supposedly in a saloon brawl in the days Otto was young and wild. It was hard to imagine now that he had ever been such.

The eye flicker told me that he didn't want to speak whatever he had to say in front of Amanda. I slipped my coat back on to hide the pistol from the occupants of the railroad car at large, excused myself, and followed him out onto the rear platform, putting us between the passenger car to which the platform was attached, and the express car just behind it.

"Well, Mr. Guardian, did you see him?" Otto asked.

"If you're talking about Punkin Jones, of course I saw him. I'm hired to see his kind, you know."

Otto grinned and slapped my shoulder in a "good boy!" way. "I knew you'd spot him!" he said. "Just thought it worth being sure of."

"He wasn't a welcome sight, but you know that already."

"A bad omen, that boy is," Otto said, suddenly dramatically somber.

"Yes. He's usually the scout. You see Punkin, and the next thing you know, the train is robbed and the Jones boys are riding away with grins on their faces and other folks' cash in their pockets."

"Can you stop it?"

"Forewarned is forearmed. I'll keep my eyes open, and if we have good fortune perhaps we can avert anything bad from happening."

Otto slapped my shoulder again, like an old patriarch proud of his grandson. "I knew you'd already have this in hand, Dylan," he said. "Mr. Guardian can be counted on."

"Otto," I said, "do me a favor. Quit calling me 'Mr. Guardian,' if you would."

"What? That offends you?"

"It doesn't offend me. It's just that, until the Colonel clarifies his attitude about publicity regarding my work, I have to err on the side of caution." Colonel Crane had already called me into his office for a 'serious discussion' of the story that had appeared in the *American Monthly Review.* Of course, since I'd had no idea it was being written and never personally talked to the writer, there wasn't much scolding the Colonel could rightly give me. In fact, I'd been able to persuade him that it was good that my Guardian status had gotten out. Robbers might be less prone to strike a train that they knew was specially guarded."

"I don't call you 'Mr. Guardian' in front of others. Just in private," Otto said.

"Yes. But if it becomes too natural and common for you to do that, you're bound to slip up sometime or another, Otto. So it's best, seems to me, for us to call each other by name."

"Good thinking, Mr. Guard . . . uh, Dylan. Sorry. I almost did it again. I'm afraid I'm losing my cleverness with age. I'll be careful from now on, though."

Just then there was a loud outcry and tumult from inside the passenger car behind us. A woman screamed. Otto was so startled he stumbled backward and almost tilted back over the platform rail. I reflexively reached for my pistol but restrained myself from drawing it. Then it was through the door and into the coach, Otto coming in behind me, but much more slowly.

The cry had come from a fleshy red-haired woman seated near the back of the passenger car. As I entered through the rear, I saw a man clambering up off the woman, and pieced together what had happened. The man had fallen atop the woman while walking down the aisle.

Then I realized that wasn't entirely accurate. I recognized the man who had fallen, and knew that what had happened had been no accident. Alvin Biggs Jr., an old and disliked professional cohort from my days in the detective agency business in St. Louis, was a worm of a man who actually made a kind of vile hobby out of groping women in public settings. "Accidentally," of course. But not really. He just managed to make it look that way. A conveniently timed stumble and fall, hands that just happened to go in the wrong direction, then "Little Alvin," as many of us had called him to distinguish him from his father, would be up and fulsomely apologizing to whatever woman he'd just taken advantage of. It was his way, his habit, and just one of several factors that made him one of the most repellent characters I'd ever known.

Talk on the grapevine was that Little Alvin was doing worse things than merely groping women by that time. The word "rape" had been thrown around after a foul incident in St. Louis. And he'd paid a price for it, even though the case had apparently been sufficiently unclear that no formal charges were ever made. His own father had relieved him of his job at the Biggs Investigation and Detection Agency of St. Louis because of it. Fired by his own father! Alvin Biggs's life was full of such misadventures and humiliations, weasel that he was.

I glanced up at Amanda. She, like most on the train, looked startled by the tumult Alvin had caused. I wondered why Alvin had not made Amanda the victim of his groping. She was by far more attractive than the homely woman he'd actually fallen upon.

The train lurched and slowed. A glance out the window revealed we were pulling into the outskirts of Gullytown. I saw young Jimmy Walsh standing on the station platform, lighting up a pipe. Jimmy was my unofficial young ear-on-the-streets assistant. Sometimes he waited for the train when he had some item of news to give me. Sometimes he waited for the train merely because he had nothing better to do for the moment.

I'd have a word with him about his smoking, as I had before many times, in vain.

I headed toward Alvin and his victim, despite a contrary impulse to go instead to secure Punkin Jones, who sat in the back of the railroad car. Punkin was part of a family gang of railroad bandits. The Jones gang was small-time compared to the James boys, Morgan Kirk, and some others, and not prone to be violent. But still they robbed trains, and typically the process began with Punkin taking a ride or two on the train being considered for robbery. He investigated the crew of the particular rail line, the kind of locks and latches on the express car, the driving habits of the engineers, and of course the security measures in place. I never figured out the need for all this research where the Jones gang was concerned, because they were strictly one-trick ponies, following the same standard pattern in almost all their robberies, regardless of differences from railroad to railroad. Rumor had it that Punkin had been selected as the scout for the gang because it was a job for which he held some innate aptitude despite his limited intelligence.

Despite his known history of robbery, I had no grounds for picking on Punkin Jones just then. He had already completed his sentences for any past crimes he had been convicted of. There was nothing illegal about riding peacefully in a railroad passenger car, which was all he'd done this day. Besides, all the attention was on Alvin Biggs and his vociferous victim, and I couldn't ignore that.

The red-haired woman, all broad face and bosom, was very nearly reversing the roles of victim and victimizer at that moment. She was out of her seat, her face right in Alvin's, finger wagging just under his nose while she hectored him about what he'd done. She knew his fall had been no accident, and told him so loudly; she could tell by the way he'd twisted as he fell, just to make sure he landed on her. Alvin, red-faced and miserable in embarrassment — a feeling surely not well known to him because there was little that could shame a shameless man — was vainly defending himself, declaring that it had indeed all been accidental, that he was sorry for it, and that a good moral fellow such as he would never intentionally take advantage of "such a fine woman" as the one shaking her finger in his face.

The finger-shaking and hectoring only intensified. As I reached the angry woman and the trembling Alvin, some wag in the rear of the train shook his own finger in the air in mimic fashion and hollered at the woman, "Hey, woman! You scolding him, or trying to pick his nose?"

The woman froze, then the accusing finger

turned toward the man who had hollered. Very crimson-faced at this point, she hollered, "You stay out of this you rude son of a *bitch!*" The words all but echoed in the car.

"Ma'am, ma'am," I said in my most placating voice. "Please calm and comport yourself. There's no cause to become vulgar in this public setting." Good Lord, I sounded like a Sunday school superintendent.

"Vulgar?" she said, turning to me. "If you want to know the meaning of 'vulgar,' you can find it in what this . . . this *bastard* did to me! Did you see it?"

"I *heard* it, ma'am. I wasn't in a position to actually see it. But I know this man, and what his habits are. So I agree with you that you were treated in a vulgar way. I simply was asking you to calm yourself enough to avoid loud profanity in a passenger car of the Gullytown line. No need to offend others simply because you yourself have been offended."

"And just who are you, sir? And why is it your business to tell me how I should react to being outraged upon this train?"

"Ma'am, my name is Dylan Curry, and I am an employee of this railroad, working in protection and security. Part of my task is to help maintain order, which is why I've intruded myself here."

"He's the Guardian!" said a man a couple of seats up. "He's the man who took four bullets while stopping this very rail line from getting robbed over a year ago, and lived to tell the tale. The robbers didn't, thanks to that pistol he hides under that coat and that keen shooting eye of his!"

"There's a story all about it in this magazine I'm reading!" declared the boy who'd been reading a three-month-old copy of the *Monthly American Review*.

"Well, I think I heard some about all that," the woman said, backing down a little. "I respect your work, then, sir. But how can it be you can gun down a gang of train robbers and still not be able to stop a . . . a . . . a vile piece of . . ."

"Ma'am . . ." I said warningly, anticipating some colorful obscenity from her as she sought to describe Alvin Biggs.

". . . a piece of *vermin* like this weasel here from putting his hands on the body of a virtuous woman!"

"Ma'am, it shouldn't have happened," I said, glad she'd kept her language within bounds. "But the fact is I had been called out to the rear platform and was not present to see Alvin do what he did. I regret that and apologize to you on behalf of the Gullytown rail line, though with the stipulation that you understand this was the fault of Alvin Biggs here, not the Gullytown line."

"Hmmph," she said. "I'm not sure that's good enough. I want a letter of apology from Col. Josiah Crane himself." She cocked a brow and looked at me like I'd just been put in my place. "I believe I deserve no less." She looked around at the other passengers. "Don't you believe I deserve such a letter?"

The passengers applauded and cheered. Just then little Alvin sought to take advantage of the distraction and slip away from the woman, but she grabbed him by the collar, slapped him so hard he yelped at a high pitch, and thereby earned herself another round of applause. This time I applauded along with the others, and Alvin gave me a hateful look.

"Ma'am, you'll have that letter," I said. I didn't have authority to make the promise, but I also didn't doubt that Colonel Crane would be glad to write it. If he didn't, I'd write it myself and sign his name to it. Anything to keep the peace and appease the passengers our rail line relied upon.

Amanda was writing hard on her notepad. She broke another pencil lead and silently mouthed an impolite word.

Otto appeared at my side, looking around the train. "Is anyone hurt?" he asked the crowd in general.

"I think I twisted my ankle a little when I fell," Little Alvin said in a voice wracked with faked pain.

I pulled back my right foot and shot it forward, kicking Alvin's left ankle. "This one?" I asked, then kicked the other, harder. "Or *this* one?"

Alvin howled and did some more groping, this time for the back of a nearby seat so that he wouldn't collapse. I had kicked nearly hard enough to break the ankles.

"Dylan!" Otto exclaimed. "This is no way to handle this situation, is it?"

"No, Otto, it isn't . . . arrest and trial and a good prison sentence would be better. This varmint belongs in a cell, as far as I'm concerned, writing letters of apology to all the women he's treated in like fashion over the years."

Those who had witnessed and heard this — almost everyone in the passenger car — applauded.

Otto stooped and looked out the window. The train was coming to a full stop.

"Gullytown!" Otto shouted in his dry little voice, moving back into official-duty mode.

"Entering Gullytown!" then he turned to Alvin and said, "You, sir, are due a visit to Mr. Myers."

"Who is Mr. Myers?" Alvin asked.

"He's town marshal of Gullytown," I said. "Very strict moral code. He'll not coddle a lecher like you."

"It was an *accident,* I tell you," Alvin said. "I wasn't trying to fall on her. You got to believe me, Dylan. If I'd aimed to fall on a woman on purpose, I'd have picked that pretty one with the notepad on her knee."

It went all over me. I held no obligations toward Amanda Seabury, but I'd be hanged if I'd let such a weasel insult her. I drew back a fist and was ready to flatten his ugly face, then thought better of doing something so blatant in front of a crowd. So I compromised and kicked him again instead, so hard that he fell down and hammered his chin painfully on the edge of a seat. The blow split the skin and blood trickled. I hoped it hurt.

"Lordy, Alvin, did I hurt you?" I said with sarcasm. "It was an accident, you know. Just an accident, like what you did to this fine woman here was an accident."

"You won't really turn me over to the marshal over all this, will you?" Alvin asked pleadingly. "I mean, you work for the railroad, Dylan. That's your jurisdiction. Marshal business ain't part of that."

"I'm also a signed-up, official deputy of the town marshal, too, Alvin," I told him. "And the law in this town has no patience with fondlers and rapists."

Alvin pulled back as though the words had slapped him physically across the face.

I noticed Amanda still writing with great intensity. Darn. She'd heard every word.

# 2

Town Marshal Myers missed his chance to meet Alvin Biggs. The scoundrel proved too slippery. And Otto contributed to Alvin's escape, unwittingly. He managed to get his hand on Alvin's arm and guide him toward the exit while I was temporarily blocked in by rising passengers. But Otto wasn't up to the task of keeping track of a prisoner. Alvin let Otto lead him as far as the step leading down to the train station platform, then with a simple wrenching movement broke himself free from the old man's feeble grasp, darted down to the platform, and loped off with surprising agility for a man who'd had his ankles so soundly kicked.

I felt like kicking myself when Alvin got away. I should have acted faster and deprived him of the opportunity to fly.

Otto apologized profusely when I came off the train. I told him it didn't much matter; the woman had been embarrassed, but not physically hurt, and I wasn't sure Alvin would have been worth all the trouble anyway.

Amanda was already out on the station platform when I disembarked. Though the weather was pleasant, she was trembling like it was a winter day. I approached her.

"Amanda, are you all right? Are you ill?"

She looked at me with eyes glistening, tears on the verge of spilling down her face. Her lip trembled along with her body. Instinctively, I reached out with my left hand to touch her shoulder, wanting to comfort her. She slowly reached across with her left arm and caressed my hand gently. It made my heart speed. Then I got a closer look at her left hand and my heart almost stopped.

She was still trembling, emotionally struggling. "Tell me what's wrong, Amanda."

A tear escaped her eye and trailed down her cheek. She seemed embarrassed and wiped it away quickly. "I'm sorry," she murmured. "It's just that man, on the train . . . the one who mistreated the loud woman."

"Did he bother you as well?"

"No . . . no, not like that. It's just that I've seen him before. In St. Louis. I think he may be following me."

I felt a chill. A slug such as Alvin, following such a beauty as Amanda.

I wasn't about to let her go out into a town where Little Alvin was roaming free, with God only knows what ill intentions. The man was a reputed rapist, after all. I told her I'd keep her company if she'd allow it.

She did. My invitation to dinner was accepted with no hesitation. She even slipped her hand in the crook of my arm and pressed against me as we walked together. Young Jimmy Walsh, boy of the streets and frequent source of information for me from the criminal underbelly of the town, passed us, no longer puffing his pipe. He eyed Amanda stealthily, then looked at me and nodded quickly, indicating his approval. Worldly-wise little fellow, Jimmy Walsh.

The Palace Restaurant stood two blocks from the train station. It was by far the best dining establishment in Gullytown. My previous meals there, however, had either been taken alone or in the company of railroad men or Marshal Myers. That evening's dining experience would far surpass them all by simple merit of the company I was in.

I kept my eyes straight ahead, not looking at the places and people around us, secure in the knowledge that any men who might happen to be watching Amanda and me were certainly envying me.

The Palace was renowned for its fish dishes and advertised FRESH SEAFOOD on its windows. "Fresh" severely punished the concept of truth. The fish served at the Palace came in by railroad, preserved by salting, in casks, or on ice. Good food, clean and safe, but hardly "fresh." I informed Amanda of this, thinking it my duty not to let her be deceived by false advertising, then regretted doing so when she informed me snippily that she was certainly not foolish, nor unaware that the nearest ocean was far from Missouri.

The coffee was hot and excellent, the bread served before the meal aromatic and steaming, and topped with delicious butter. I could have easily gorged myself like a foundering heifer, but in the presence of my lovely companion took pains to be on my most gentlemanly behavior. I took fastidious little bites.

Amanda, meanwhile, ate with the un-self-conscious abandon of a hungry little girl. Yet she managed to do it with a certain dignity.

The paper tablet she'd written on in the train appeared from the big, soft carpetbag purse she carried and found its place on the table. She quickly flipped pages and found the first available blank one. Then a pencil came out of the bag, she licked the lead, and it was time for the interview to resume. I still wasn't sure why.

"Let me just ask you straight out, so there is no question about it — you truly are the 'Guardian' figure who was the subject of Joseph Myerson's recent story in the *Monthly American Review*. Am I correct?"

"Well, I don't know this Myerson name you said. I don't recall who wrote that story. But yes, I'm the one the story was about."

"Was it an accurate story?"

"It was accurate," I said. "I have no complaint about it other than the fact I was completely surprised to find myself the subject of a national magazine story when I was never even approached by the writer of it. Everything he wrote he got from talking to other people."

She looked at me as if I were distressingly ignorant. "One thing that must be kept in mind in those kinds of situations is the fact that the working press can hardly ask permission before writing stories that are of value and public interest. Now, it would be one thing if Myerson had interviewed you personally, without explaining his reason, and published a story *based on that interview* without your permission. But I take it that is not what he did. He spoke to others about your heroism in halting a train robbery and actually wiping out the gang who was carrying it out."

"They almost wiped me out first. Four bullet wounds, two potentially deadly, the other two almost costing me an arm."

"I saw the scars of the latter two when you rolled up your sleeve on the train today."

"Every time I see those scars I'm reminded of how close I came to death that day. It's a dangerous job I've undertaken, this Guardian task. Sometimes I wonder if I was wise to take it at all."

"Dylan, I say this with the utmost sincerity: I believe that you, in your unique role, have the potential to become a legendary figure in this country, as some of our frontier peace officers are doing, or such men as the late Crockett and Boone. I mean that."

"Fame isn't the point. The point is the safety of the railroad. My employer, Col. Josiah Crane, had mixed feelings about the publication of that story. But he liked the ring of the Guardian name. He's now hung it upon me as an informal title. Officially I am simply labeled 'security agent.' But in actual practice am usually referred to as the

Guardian. More drama in that name, I suppose, than just calling me a guard or security officer."

"And no other rail line in America possesses an employee with a similar designation."

"None to my knowledge. There are security officers on railroads across America, but to my knowledge I am the only one hired because of past associations with . . . uh, the *other side* of the railroad robbery issue."

She grinned broadly and wrote with enthusiasm on her pad. I could see that she believed she was onto something noteworthy. But I could not believe that she would have much luck persuading the *Monthly American Review* to publish another piece of journalism even indirectly about me, given how recently Myerson's had run. And curious as I was about what she would write, I didn't really want to see another article done. Excessive publicity about my work on the Gullytown line might have the effect of averting potential robbers from attacking that line, it was true . . . but on the other hand, I knew personally many of the individuals who robbed trains in this part of the nation. Some of them would see my roll as the Guardian as a nose-thumbing challenge. Virtually an invitation for them to prove to the world I wasn't such a hero and protector after all.

I'd nearly been killed by one gaggle of thieves already. I didn't want to attract others who might want to see if they could complete the job that others had failed to complete.

Amanda glanced to the side, looking out the front window of the restaurant. She gasped suddenly and seemed to freeze.

"What's wrong?" I asked.

"He's out there. He was looking through the window at me!"

"Who?"

"You know. *Him* . . . the man from the train." Her lip trembled. "Alvin Biggs."

I looked and saw no one. Maybe Alvin had just passed by the window quickly.

"Amanda, are you sure?" I asked.

"Yes. Yes, I know that ugly face. I've seen it too many times, in St. Louis, and now here. There's no question in my mind that he's following me."

"Do you know why?"

She hesitated, then said, "Yes. I think so."

I, of course, was thinking of Alvin's reputed status as a rapist, and wondering if he was following her because he'd established her as his next target. Maybe she was thinking the same thing. This conversation had the potential to become quite delicate.

"Can you tell me why he's following you?" I ventured.

"Yes. He wants to kill me. He's been hired to do it."

I gaped. "Are you sure?"

"I am, yes."

"Lord above, Amanda, who would want to kill you?" I said it low to avoid being heard by others dining nearby. And just as I asked the question I found my eyes drawn again to the third finger of her left hand. She noticed it and quickly dropped her hand below the edge of the table, hiding it.

I asked a question I would later realize was quite rude and intrusive, at least by the standards of the region and the times. But my motivation was good: a simple desire to understand the truth of her situation. "Amanda, is it divorce or separation? Or are you a widow?"

The questions unsettled her and a frown darkened her pretty features. "I beg your pardon, sir?"

Obviously I'd offended her. "Amanda, I can see the impressions of your rings upon your left-hand ring finger. Until recently you've worn rings, and now you've removed them. Truly, I'm not trying to intrude into

50

your personal life, Amanda, but you've told me a remarkable thing: Someone wants you dead. I have to wonder if that someone is a husband you have separated from or divorced."

She looked embarrassed, upset. Her eyes brimmed, but she fought it. She looked at her ring finger and studied the marks I'd referred to. "I never thought about such a small thing giving me away," she said.

"Before my current work for the raiload, I was an investigative criminal detective in St. Louis. I was trained to look for small details and evaluate them. Most folks might not have noticed those ring marks, or thought about them. But I've been taught to look for such things."

She nodded and looked at the window again, fear in her eyes.

"Amanda, I was rude in asking you such a blunt question. But I want to help you, and to do that I need to know exactly what you're facing."

She slumped and looked deflated and somber. "I can't lie, Dylan. And you've caught me anyway, so what's the point of trying? Yes, I was a married woman . . . until recently."

I waited for her to continue, but she merely stared at the tabletop. "Amanda, are you widowed?" I ventured.

She looked at me with a sad face. Slowly she shook her head. "I'm sorry to have to tell you this, because you may be one of those who finds it scandalous, but the fact is that I'm divorced."

"I see."

"Do you think I'm scandalous, then?"

"Scandalous? No. Just unfortunate in marriage. It happens to a lot of people, good people."

She seemed honestly relieved to hear me say it. I saw relaxation come over her features, and suddenly she was pretty again. She'd lost a little of that when she'd looked so dejected.

I'd been intrusive already, so why stop now? "Amanda, is your former husband the one trying to have you killed?"

She looked sad again. "I think so."

What do you say to someone in such a situation? The moment was uncomfortable, but mercifully, the waiter arrived with the meals we'd ordered. Fish for both of us, even if we knew it wasn't actually fresh. It was good, though, and provided a distraction from a rather grim conversation.

"You are from Tennessee, I think?" she asked. Now that she was eating, she didn't seem so nervous and dejected. "I think the

*Review* story about you said you were from Tennessee . . . and you sound like it. I'm familiar with the accent. I once had a beau from Tennessee, you see."

I wondered if she'd like to have another, but didn't voice the thought.

"Which part of the state are you from?" she asked, and the notepad and pencil came back into play again.

"Right from the middle of the state. Calfkiller River area."

"That's an odd name, 'Calfkiller.' What does it come from?"

"There's a lot of stories. Most of them guesswork, I think. Some say it was the name of an Indian chief who used to be there. I've heard as well that it comes from a flood that once killed some cattle. Truth is, I don't know."

She wrote diligently. "I still don't fully understand the need for all these notes," I said.

"It's simply an aid for memory. Pay no attention to it. But tell me: how did you fall in with the kind of men who fought as irregulars and guerillas and ended up robbing trains and such?"

"It was the war," I replied. "Tennessee went with the Rebellion, but it was a much-divided state. Union and Confederate living side by side, sometimes getting along well enough, other times killing one another, killing each other's kin, burning farms and houses. A lot of partisan bands rose up. Bushwhackers, regulators, and the like. Ever heard of Champ Ferguson? Tinker Dave Beatty? Dave Bowington?"

"Yes," she replied, sipping at her teacup. "Wasn't one of them hanged after the war?"

"Two. Ferguson and Bowington were hanged. No pardons for them. They were considered criminals, not legitimate soldiers. They were tried in Nashville, separate trials, then sent to the gallows, one dying a month before the other. Ferguson first."

"Go back earlier. What did you do during the war?"

"I rode with Bowington while I was in Tennessee. I admit I took part in some of the things he did, including robbing some trains. Then I met up with a fellow from Missouri who had moved down to Tennessee before the war to take up farming land he inherited from his people. But he got a notion to go back home to Missouri when he got word there was so much trouble there and in Kansas. And by the time he was ready to go, I'd seen some things done by Bowington that made me want to get away from him. So I went off to Missouri, too. And started riding with Parsons' Raiders."

She looked at me so oddly I wondered if I'd just sprouted a third ear. "Jim Parsons? The outlaw Jim Parsons?"

"The very man. Train and bank robber of extraordinary skill . . . better at his kind of work than the Jameses, lots say, and meaner."

"You rode with him."

"During the war, yes. Afterward, only for a little while. I found I couldn't stay with it. I could live with being a soldier, even an irregular, during wartime. But I couldn't live with being an outright outlaw once the war was over. It went against my raising. So I left Parsons behind once he decided to continue his activities after the surrender was signed."

"What about Morgan Kirk?"

"What about him?"

"Didn't you ride with him some after the war?

I shook my head firmly. "Not Kirk, no. I encountered him a time or two, but never rode with him. I was never part of his gang."

She looked as though she didn't believe me. She also seemed quite disappointed. "Never?" she asked. "Because my mentor Brannigan talked to Myerson, who wrote the story about you, and he says that Myerson told him you'd once been part of Kirk's gang."

"Myerson misunderstood, then. Good thing he didn't put that into his story — he'd have heard from me if he had. Keep in mind that I was part of Parsons' gang, and Kirk and Parsons were rivals. Hated each other."

"Whether you rode with Kirk or not, you did have knowledge of what went on among the outlaws and renegades of the border."

"That's correct."

"How much did you know of Kirk?"

"Just the usual stories."

"Any truth to those stories?"

"It would depend on what stories you were talking about. There were lies and legends told about Kirk, Parsons, the James boys, the Youngers, Bloody Bill, all of them. Amanda, why are you so interested in Morgan Kirk in particular?"

"I'm trying to find lore, tales of the people. Material that makes for good reading, good journalism. That's all. Material I can perhaps build a career for myself with. And there are aspects of the lore regarding Morgan Kirk that particularly fascinate me." I had the strongest sense that things were going unsaid, that there was much more to the story than she was telling.

I dived in. "Lots of stories are told about him. A lot having to do with hidden loot from his crimes. Hidden treasure stories. Not much different than the old 'lost silver mine' tales that come up all over the country."

She lifted her head and stared at me down her perfect nose. I'd never seen such haughtiness on a feminine face. "I'm *not* looking for hidden treasure, if that is your insinuation. I have my own reasons for wanting to meet Morgan Kirk. Professional reasons that I've already told you about."

"He's a very dangerous man."

"I'm aware of that. Tell me something, Dylan: can you lead me to Morgan Kirk?"

"I have no special connection to the man. Don't want one. But I'd know him if I saw him. And I know where he can be found when he's in these parts."

"Tell me one more thing: is he scarred?"

"Scarred?"

"Yes. There are stories that he suffered terrible scarring after an inept doctor did surgery on his face a few years ago."

"I've heard that, but don't know many details. Was he trying to change his appearance to make it easier to hide from the law?"

"It's not a pleasant thing to discuss at a

meal, I know, but the story I hear is that he was afflicted with cancers of the skin. He wanted them removed, and they *were* removed, but the surgeon was incompetent and drunk and did great damage to his appearance. Supposedly he even used strong acid to burn off some of the cancers, and carved out others with a blade. Horrible story, I know. The end result was that Morgan Kirk's face was ruined, and he now hides it behind a cloth mask much of the time."

"What became of the doctor afterward?"

"I don't know."

"From what I know of Kirk, I'm betting that doctor didn't live to practice bad medicine on anyone else. Kirk isn't the kind to abide a wrong done to him."

She drew in her breath and regained that haughty look I'd noticed before. "I've heard that about him. And I admire that aspect of the man. He understands the idea of repayment . . . of giving evil for evil. Of doing what must be done. Yes."

I looked at my dinner companion without knowing how to reply to that. The things she was saying now hinted at deeper and perhaps darker aspects within this young woman than were evident on the pretty surface.

"Amanda, why do you want to meet Morgan Kirk? It's a kind of ambition one doesn't expect to find in a young woman." She'd probably find the question repetitive and annoying, but she'd not given me an answer yet that I could fully believe.

"I explained this already," she said. "I am a journalist of American lore. And he is a source and subject of American lore. Is there any surprise I would want to meet him?"

"Yes, considering how wicked a man he is. Not many people wish to associate with murderers."

"What is murder to one is justice to another. You know Kirk's motto, don't you? It's rather famous. 'Betrayal brings death.' I like that. It has a firm, solid ring to it. 'Betrayal brings death.' "

I had nothing to say to that. Just to fill the silence, I stammered out the obvious: "So . . . when it's all said, you want to meet Morgan Kirk so you can write about him."

"It would be quite a tale to tell, you must admit."

She was right about that, and I admitted so. "He's a wanted man. I know he's suspected in a train derailment over in Colorado earlier this year, and possibly in some others."

"I've heard the same."

"Odd thing is, the train that was derailed wasn't robbed. It was a commissioned short-run train, no real cargo, but it included a private coach car bearing a banker named Ferrell who was traveling into a little town for some reason or another."

"He was going there to tell his wife that he was leaving her," she said.

"How do you know that?"

"I've talked to people, that's all. Myerson, for one. Myerson wrote about the Colorado derailment. The same Myerson who wrote about you. Myerson told me personally that the belief is that Ferrell was killed by someone hired by his wife, to whom he'd reportedly been unfaithful."

"And the hired killer was Kirk."

"That, at least, is the rumor. I'd like to find the truth. I've heard it was actually his gunman Ben Menko who killed Ferrell."

"If so, he did it on behalf of Kirk, and at his behest. I've met Menko. He's a devil of a man, maybe worse than Kirk himself in ways. But he's a follower, not a leader. And loyal to Kirk to the end."

She was clearly impressed that I knew such a human demon as Ben Menko. I went on: "Kirk has been reported seen recently in the vicinity of Gryner Hill, a few miles northwest from here. His mother, quite an old woman now, has lived there for years. But I assume you already knew that."

"Yes."

"If you do ever meet Kirk, I'd advise you not to ask him about Ferrell. I don't think it would be a well-received question."

"A journalist must be bold."

"Sounds to me like the kind of journalism you practice is more or less gossip."

"Is that intended to insult me, Dylan?"

"Not at all. It is just an observation. I don't pretend to understand journalism and such. All I know of journalism is the local paper, really just a rag that's run by a fellow named Ralph Wiles . . . kind of a skinny little wide-eyed fellow in glasses who seems determined to see me as the biggest hero since George Washington. His version of my story is not far short of having me not only shoot down that gang myself, but pick the whole dang train up and carry it into town on my shoulders, passengers and all."

"Clearly your local paper could use some improvement. Or some competition. But to go back to what you said before, about not understanding journalism. Obviously you don't. There's much more than 'gossip' to good journalism. A good journalist does not merely repeat rumors in print. One picks up those rumors from talking to people, and listening to them, and then one investigates to find out what the truth is."

"I may not understand journalism, but I do understand investigation, Amanda. I did it for a living in St. Louis, and in fact still do, both in my work for the railroad and my work with the town marshal."

"You work with the town marshal's office as well as the railroad?"

"Didn't you read Myerson's story? It was in there. I'm an officially sworn-in deputy of Marshal Myers. Having deputy status allows me to legally carry a pistol on my person while in Gullytown, and to make arrests not just as a citizen but as a badge-carrying officer of the law."

She had a thoughtful look. "So you are a man of the law. Sworn to follow it."

"I am."

She ate in silence a few moments, then looked up at me frankly. "Do you believe there are two levels of law?"

"I'm not sure what you mean."

"I mean, do you believe there is law written on law books, but also a law written in nature, in the world itself? And that the two levels of law might not always be the same?"

I was unsure what she was getting at. "If you mean, do I believe there is a law of right and wrong independent of what people say, yes, I do believe that."

"And could there be situations in which the kind of law that is made up by human beings and written down in law books could fail to match up to the independent 'law of right and wrong,' as you called it . . . the unwritten law?"

"I suppose there is such a thing as bad human law. People write laws and people can make mistakes."

"And in such situations, which law should someone follow, the written law or the unwritten law?"

What the devil was this all about? I had to admit, though, she was waking me up some, making me think.

"It might depend on how bad the bad law was. If it was a small matter, I suppose the prudent thing to do would be to go ahead and just follow the written law and avoid trouble. But if it was big enough, and important, I suppose you'd have to follow the unwritten higher law." I stopped, but she looked at me as if waiting for me to continue. "That's what we fought a war over a few years ago, when you think about it," I said. "The Southern folk felt like the Federal government was using its written law to take away rights for states to decide their own ways, which they saw as one of those higher laws you talked about. So they rebelled and defied the immediate law and did what they thought was right in the bigger sense. They followed the higher law as they saw it. Or tried to."

"And the same with those on the other side," Amanda said. "There were some of us who could not accept that it was right to enslave other human beings, regardless of what was written in our laws. It was a violation of the unwritten law of nature to have man-made laws that allowed for slavery."

"So you were an outright abolitionist on the matter of slavery."

"I was. I was just a little girl, following her instincts as I listened to the adults talk and argue and make war on each other."

"For what it's worth, Amanda, I've never favored slavery, either. Neither did my father, even though he was a staunch Confederate. The reason he went the way he did in the war was that he was a stubborn sort who didn't like the notion of uppity Yankees dictating to our kind of folk how we had to live and think. Me, I went along with his point of view because he was my father. There was a lot more to that war than just slavery."

"Bottom of it all, it was slavery that put

the edge on the knife, and you have to admit it. It was because of slavery that you folks cared so much about your precious 'states' rights.' Can you deny that?"

"Yeah, I can deny it. There was just much more to that fight than the question of slavery, whatever you think."

"I suppose I can understand that point of view, if I try," Amanda said. "But I didn't mean for us to get off on a philosophical discussion. I want to hear your story, how you went from being a backwater boy to a unique Guardian on a Missouri railroad line."

"I learned a lot of hard lessons in war while I was still back home," I said. "I never did favor a nation of people fighting between themselves, and never did put on a uniform. I just rode with Bowington's Confederate irregulars. Never with Ferguson, though. Ferguson was too hard a man for me."

"Why did they hang Bowington after the war?"

"Partly because of me. I testified in his trial . . . against him. Testified to things I'd seen him do."

"What had he done?"

I paused a long and solemn while before answering. "Wrong things. And not just the normal wrongs of war, either, but things that didn't have to be done, but which he did for his own reasons. Robbery, theft, pillage, murder, rape. Most of it with little or nothing to do with the wartime cause. You see, down in that part of the country, just like here, there were plenty who used the war as an excuse to do what they wanted, to get their own revenge against people they hated long before the thing turned into a war. Bowington was that way. And it finally got so I couldn't bear to associate with him anymore. I wanted out, away from him. That's why I came to Missouri when I got the chance. And I haven't been back to Tennessee since but for two times. The most recent was to bury my father. My mother died before the war commenced. The other visit, next-to-the-last one, was some years before that, to give testimony in Bowington's trial in Nashville."

"You are a fortunate man," she said.

"How so? I was just telling you of the deaths of my parents."

"Yes . . . but when you speak of them I can tell you had a good life with them. So you are fortunate. I never had a real chance to know my own parents."

"I'm sorry."

She steered the interview back on course before I could question her more about her family. "You said you testified against Bowington. You turned against the kinds of things Bowington did. But what was the difference in joining yourself to a man like Parsons?"

"There's not much I can say to that. There was little difference, in fact."

"So you hold Parsons in low regard as well?"

"The man himself I found easy to like. But the things he *did* were a different matter. I can't favor robbing trains and banks and such. I'm on the other side of all that now that the war is done, and he should be, too. When a war ends, so should the war-making."

"But think of the fame you could have if you still worked with him!"

"From all I've ever heard, fame is shallow as a street puddle," I replied. "I've known some men who have been famous, and it has been a burden on them. And if it's fame I'm after, I seem to be finding it, want it or not. All you journalists seem to want to write about me."

I had the strongest feeling that all this discussion, random as it seemed, had a point known only to Amanda Seabury. I didn't think she was likely to explain herself, though, without prompting.

"Amanda, may I be forthright with you?"

"I wish you would."

"I want to know why you are so interested in my past associations with men now known as criminals. What, precisely, do you want from me?"

She shrugged and began paying more attention to her food. She wasn't so much a fast eater as a steady one, and her plate was empty well before mine was. She laid down her fork.

"What do I want from you?" she asked. "Coffee. And dessert. Apple pie would do nicely."

It did. Amanda had two slices. Quite an appetite! Just one more interesting and unexpected thing about this unusual and extraordinarily beautiful young woman.

She took a sip of coffee and poised her pencil above that ever-present notepad.

"How did you go from wartime associate of various irregulars and bushwhackers to your current role with the railroad?"

"It goes back to the war, really," I replied. "It was while I was with Parsons. There was a train that needed stopping, and a Union officer aboard who it was our goal to capture. That's what Parsons told us, anyway. So we stopped that train. The railroad ran through a steep-sided gap. We filled it up with logs and trees, and made that train stop. And once we got on board, it didn't take long to find out what Parsons was really after."

"Not the officer?"

"No. The officer's daughter. Name of Katrina Crane. A very beautiful young lady, like you."

"Why did he want her?"

I paused. This was a delicate matter to discuss with a young woman. "Amanda, Jim Parsons is the same kind of man as Alvin Biggs, in ways. Except worse, I think. His intentions toward Katrina Crane were . . . carnal. He intended to take the worst kind of advantage of her. I'm sorry to speak so immodestly to you, but it is the truth. Jim Parsons stopped that train to get his hands on the beautiful daughter of Col. Josiah Crane. She was traveling with her father. Colonel Crane's presence provided a convenient way for Parsons to instigate his men to help him . . . for not one of us would have helped Parsons stop that train if we'd known we were doing so in order for him to commit an outrage on an innocent young woman. Capturing a Federal officer we would gladly do. Aiding and abetting the molestation of a woman, no. So he used the

69

capture of Colonel Crane as a pretext to maintain the loyalty of his men until he could get what he really wanted."

Amanda blanched a little.

The next portion of the story I could feel prouder to tell. "Katrina Crane never suffered the fate Parsons had in mind for her. Colonel Crane and I had a chance to whisper to each other a bit, and after the train was stopped and he and his associates were disarmed, when I saw what Parsons was actually up to, I slipped a pistol back to Colonel Crane. Together we saved Katrina from being misused."

Amanda's admiring look felt like warm sun against my face. "That's good," she said. "Very good."

"Yes. But it brought something bad to Colonel Crane. He and Parsons fought on the train. Hand to hand. The train began to move again. They ended up on a little platform between two cars . . . and then they fell."

"Oh, no! *Under* the train?"

"Partly."

"Anyone killed?"

"Neither man. But both were badly hurt. Especially Colonel Crane. He lost both legs. Below the knees. Parsons lost his left leg above the ankle, and his left arm at the elbow. Both men lived through it all."

"What a horrible story!"

"It doesn't end there. That event led to other things for me, including the life I have now. Parsons, you see, blamed me for what happened because I was the one who slipped a gun to Colonel Crane. And he cursed at me, by name, when they were hauling him away to get his wounds tended. So Colonel Crane learned who I was from hearing Parsons call my name."

She was intrigued at this point, listening so closely she was taking fewer notes. "What happened next?"

"I got away from Parsons at first opportunity, to begin with. Just left his little army of bushwhackers behind, and managed to make it through the remainder of the war without getting dragged in again. But I stayed in the Midwest. Didn't want to go back down South, not the way things were there at that time. Fortunately, my name and face had never gotten well known during my time with Parsons, so I was just another unknown face instead of being a wanted outlaw. I found honest work, though at first it was just low-level things like tending a bar, working in a stable, blacksmithing a bit . . . and then I went to work in St. Louis as a policeman. That didn't last long, but I learned a lot. Skills of detection in particular. I also learned that I didn't much like working for the public, though I did well at it. Then fate stepped in again. One particular day, during the time I was still a policeman but thinking about getting away from it, I was riding on a little spur line railroad, and happened to see some of my old companions from the Parsons days, some of them on the train. Then looking ahead out a window, I saw others of them situated outside it. I recognized the setup. That train was about to be robbed, and I could see it coming. It happened that the president of that little rail line was on that train that day. I learned who he was and told him what was about to happen. He had the train go on past its stop and that rob-bery never happened. But some of Parsons' old boys got frustrated and angry, and fired some shots at the train, so it was pretty clear that I hadn't been just spouting nonsense when I told them there was going to be a robbery. That railroad president made sure to get my name, and I didn't mind sharing it with him. I had a feeling it could lead to something."

The next portion of the story proved of particular interest to Amanda Seabury. She leaned over her plate and gazed at me with a new intensity when I began to talk of the one young woman in my life I had loved — Jerusha Hannibal.

I told her how I'd met Jerusha at a little café I frequented in my policeman days. She operated a little dress shop next door, and often we ended up at the café at the same time. One crowded day we shared a table, the first time of many more times to come. Before long we were sharing tables at other restaurants, after hours, and visiting theaters, musical performances, even lectures. It was an educational romance for me, literally so. Jerusha was a young woman of intense curiosity and abundant mental energy, and at one point even persuaded me, who had had only the most minimal schooling, to join her in sitting through a week's worth of classes in a small college, studying the early history of the nation. I spent most of the class time staring at her, only half listening to the professor. I did pick up enough knowledge to develop a new appreciation for the nation that was my home, and to allow myself to question whether the Confederate rebellion of which I had been a part had been right-minded.

I told Amanda how my relationship with Jerusha also led to another relationship: friendship with her brother, Mark. Though the romance with Jerusha was not to last, the friendship with Mark Hannibal did. Long after the time Jerusha told me that I was not the man for her after all, breaking my heart, my friendship with her brother went on. Then came a crucial turn of events. Mark Hannibal signed on with a private detective agency in St. Louis, and I soon received an invitation to do the same. Weary of police work, I accepted the job. Though detective work was not terribly dissimilar from what I'd done as a policeman, the fact it was private work, not public duty, appealed. I was ready for a change.

It was a wise move. I thrived as a detective, and through a combination of hard work, competence, and luck solved some cases on behalf of notable and wealthy clients. One of them, perchance, was a railroad official, a talkative one who spoke of me to another man who was launching a Midwestern railroad line. Thanks to a recent inheritance that other man was a wealthy investor, a decorated veteran of the war who had literally given part of himself for the American Union. He was the former colonel, Josiah Crane, the same man whose daughter I had helped save from atrocious treatment by Jim Parsons during that earlier train robbery.

Colonel Crane remembered me. And when Crane launched his own railroad line, the Gullytown-Cheruka Rail Line, usually simply called the Gullytown Line, he decided that my skills, and those of the agency for which Mark Hannibal and I worked, might be useful to his new enterprise.

But initially Crane did not hire the agency. The owner of the agency was a former Confederate sympathizer who lacked the couth to keep his views to himself, and this offended Colonel Crane and cost the agency a major and extended engagement in railroad security.

The Colonel might have been better off to have ignored the uncouth employer and hired the agency despite him, I explained to Amanda. The Gullytown Line quickly began to fall victim to robberies, especially after it became public knowledge that it frequently hauled gold and cash. The robbers who plagued the line like hornets were identified as former Confederate raiders who were continuing their wartime exploits into the postwar era. Among them were, reportedly, members of what was now called the Parsons Gang, formerly Parsons' Raiders.

"Eventually," I said to Amanda, "Colonel Crane reconsidered his decision. But even then he did not hire the agency as a whole.

Instead he came to me personally, and told me he wanted to hire me, individually, as a security officer for his railroad. Later, perhaps, he would allow me to hire assistants, if I wished. But for now, it was me alone."

"And so you became the Guardian," Amanda said.

"I became the Guardian."

# 3

Amanda had given Otto Bracken a couple of dollars to go to the hotel for her and reserve a room on the third floor. She'd insisted on the third floor. Otto had spent one of the dollars to subcontract out to a local boy the task of hauling Amanda's bags to the hotel. He was a little too old to haul heavy carpetbags up three floors.

After the meal I walked her as far as the beginning of the third-floor hallway.

"Thank you for dinner, Dylan," she said, extending her hand quite properly.

I took that hand and looked her in the face. "Amanda, I worry that you won't be safe here alone and with Alvin Biggs running around loose in town. I wish you had someone to be with you tonight."

I winced inwardly. What I'd said sounded way too forward and implied something I hadn't intended. But she didn't look shocked or offended.

"I'll be fine," she said. "I'll lock myself in and not let anyone enter. Nobody is going to try to get to me in such a public setting as a hotel."

"You seem very confident for someone who didn't seem confident at all a couple of hours ago."

She smiled and shrugged.

If she felt confident of her safety, I didn't. Not with such rapacious vermin as Little Alvin Biggs on the streets.

I said my good-night to her, shook her hand, and waited at the end of the hallway until she was safe in her room, whose number I mentally noted. Then I left, knowing that before the evening was over I'd be back, probably more than once, to make sure nothing was amiss.

The darkness had brought in a mild chill. I pulled my jacket a little closer around me and trudged across the street, through an alleyway, down another street a few paces, then through a second alley toward the railroad. I had a room, not in the hotel, but in a boardinghouse elsewhere in town. But I wasn't ready to go there yet.

Only a few people were around the train, railroad and freight workers unloading boxcars by the light of streetlamps. I spoke to several I knew as I walked by, then reached an empty boxcar with cargo doors partly open. I climbed up inside, then sat down on the edge of the boxcar floor, feet dangling out the door. I found a cigar in my jacket pocket, one forgotten about and by pure luck left unbroken and uncrushed. I bit off the tip end and fired up. The cigar was cheap and strong, biting the tongue — the kind I liked.

The night thickened. The workmen finished their tasks and headed off for suppers and cigars of their own. Before long I was alone.

I threw the cigar butt under the train and by the illumination of the streetlamps strode up and down the cargo platform, thinking about Amanda Seabury. I rounded the back of the train and walked up its length again. Halfway up the line of boxcars, I heard something bump inside one of them. A human-sounding kind of bump. Someone was in there.

The cargo door of the particular boxcar from which the noise had come was closed on the side I was passing, so I slipped between cars, climbed over the coupling, and went to the other side. The door on that side was open, just enough to accommodate a man.

I reached under my jacket and pulled my

small revolver from the shoulder holster there, then listened closely. No noise from inside the boxcar now. I lost confidence that anyone was in there. Saying a little prayer just in case, I went to the open cargo door and peered into the boxcar. Nothing at first . . . then motion. But low to the floor, not movement at a level one would expect if caused by a human being.

I stuck my head through the door and got a better view. A cat. That's all it was. Just a cat.

Relieved I wouldn't have to deal with an intruder after all, I pulled my head back out and slipped the pistol into its holster as I turned, chuckling at myself for having gotten all worked up over nothing. I caught a glimpse of rapid motion behind me, something descending fast, a face twisted in anger and exertion . . . then something struck my head, ringing my skull like a clapper on a bell. Everything became muddled; the man who had struck me had two faces now, identical and familiar. My eyes refused to draw those faces together into one. He hit again, and all was darkness.

I began to come around a few seconds later. On the ground beside the track, almost up against one of the big steel wheels, I rolled over and opened my eyes. I saw only one image of my attacker this time, but there was a second figure behind him, creeping up with a board in hand. My attacker leaned down and looked at me with the kind of grimacing, triumphant smile only a face as ugly as that of Alvin Biggs could generate — and just then Amanda Seabury, who had managed to sneak up behind him, brought down the board in her hand onto the back of his skull.

He grunted loudly when Amanda's board made contact, then collapsed atop me, his chin striking my shoulder and causing him to bite his tongue. Still in his hands was the stick he had used to strike me before Amanda had struck Alvin in turn. Blood ran down his chin and stained my shirt. I was groggy and my head ached, but I wasn't inclined to be bled on. "Get off me, Little Alvin!" I shoved him up and away, and Alvin rolled off and flopped out on the earth between the train and the platform, a limp and groaning human mass.

I managed to get up and onto the platform, then felt dizzy. I staggered, bumping against Amanda. In part of my jangled brain I found enough lingering rationality to wonder how Amanda had happened to be where she was, and why she'd risked her own safety by intervening on my behalf. I staggered again and she grabbed me, keeping me from falling.

"Dylan, can you stand? Can you walk?"

"Amanda . . . why . . . why did you follow me?"

"We'll talk about it later. For now just be glad that I did. I didn't know we'd find this piece of filth lingering around. He hit you hard, Dylan."

"I know . . . you hit . . . him . . . hard, too." It was hard to talk clearly.

"I did, didn't I!" She beamed like a happy child and chuckled. "I guess I showed *him,* huh?"

"Is he alive?"

Her hand tightened on my arm. "Good God, do you think I hit him hard enough to kill him?"

She went to where Little Alvin lay senseless beside the train. I stood still, yet felt inside my throbbing skull like I was turning circles. Alvin had walloped my head powerfully. Revenge, I supposed, for how I'd treated Alvin during the earlier incident on the train.

Amanda returned. "He's out cold, but still alive," she said. "I'm glad I hit him."

"He is a loathsome little creature. I'll grant you that. And a hired killer, too, if what you've told me is right."

She glared down at the unmoving man. "Maybe I should have hit him even harder. Killed him."

"Amanda, why did you leave your room and follow me? I had no idea you'd done it until I saw you sneaking up behind Alvin."

"I . . . I was nervous, being in the hotel alone. I thought about what you said, how I shouldn't stay there by myself. Every creak and thump I heard began to scare me. I looked out the window and saw you over here near the train . . . on the third floor, you have a good, far-ranging perspective . . . and I saw you walking around, smoking a cigar. It looked like you, anyway, from that distance. Then I saw somebody behind you, creeping along, sort of . . . and I just had to come and see what was going on. I'm glad I did."

"So am I."

"Where do you live?" she asked. "We must get you off your feet."

"Boardinghouse," I said. "I'll show you."

Gullytown was not a big town, but the walk across it to my boardinghouse seemed to take forever. The company was good, though. Amanda stayed close by my side, actually holding to me most of the time.

"What about Biggs?" she asked worriedly. "He's still lying back there. Should we get the law?"

"I *am* the law," I reminded her. "For now, I say leave him where he is. He'll come around soon. And if he doesn't . . ." I paused long enough to consult my pocket-watch. "In ten minutes a watchman comes on duty at the rail station. He patrols all around, and he'll find Alvin if he's still there. He'll probably figure him to be a drunk who passed out, not somebody who got knocked out, but he'll deal with him in whatever case. His name is Bert Rader, and he's a part-time deputy of the town marshal, just like me. He can handle Alvin."

Mrs. Finch's boardinghouse was in a large, classic house painted in a color something between yellow and the palest of browns. Mrs. Finch was a woman of extraordinary neatness and with a fondness for flowers and decoration, and Amanda responded at once to the attractive place, exclaiming over this feature and that as she led me inside and up the stairs. Mrs. Finch was out at the moment, and at present I was the only boarder, so we encountered no one else as we headed to my room.

As I fumbled out my key in the hallway, an inspiration struck. "Amanda, I've got an idea. There's empty rooms here, and Mrs. Finch is looking for boarders. Why don't

84

you talk to her tomorrow and see if you can become one? That way you can be right here in this same building, and I can feel more confident of your safety because I'll be close by to watch over you."

She looked intrigued, but maybe a little offended, too. "Do you think I'm looking for a protector, Dylan? That I need Guardian services just like the railroad?"

"If your former husband is trying to have you killed, then, yes, I'd say you are a candidate for protection. I mean no offense in saying that."

She nodded. "I'm sorry. I'm too sensitive, I suppose. Ever since I was a little girl I've had an independent streak and despised the notion that I can't take care of myself. The idea of needing a protector doesn't sit easily with me."

I got the door open and we entered the room. She didn't hesitate to go inside, even though it wasn't considered a "proper" thing for a lone woman to be in the bed-chamber of a single man. Not that there was anyone to see us at the moment and pass judgment . . . but Mrs. Finch might return from wherever she was at any point, and if she found a woman in my room, judgment would definitely be passed. Mrs. Finch was a very moral type and insisted on high standards of behavior in her boardinghouse.

"I like your room," Amanda said, walking around. "Is the bed comfortable? I'm asking, of course, in case I do decide to rent a room here. I can't abide a place with uncomfortable beds."

"The bed is fine," I said. "I assume they are equally good in the other rooms."

She went to the window and peered out around the edge of the curtain, keeping herself hidden behind it. She was being careful, I supposed, because of the danger she was in. Or maybe she was looking out for my reputation, so that none of the local wags would begin quizzing me about why a beautiful young woman was seen in the window of my room.

"I hope you will rent a room here," I told her. "How long do you anticipate being in town?"

She turned away from the window. "I'm doing some business here," she said. "I'm not sure how long it will take. I'll be in town a few days."

Business, she had said. I wondered what kind of business it was. "Mrs. Finch has rented rooms for as short a term as two weeks," I told her. "And her rates are reasonable."

"For now, I need to be at the hotel," she

said. "On the hotel, third floor specifically. That's where I've told my . . . prospective business associates they could find me."

A distressing thought arose. What kind of "business" could involve a young woman in a hotel room, a young woman who obviously had told certain "prospective business associates" that she would be on a particular floor of a particular hotel during a particular stretch of time? She was young, beautiful, attractive to men. And something had broken up her marriage. Could it be the kind of "business" she was operating?

Could it be? God, I hoped not. I did not want to believe Amanda Seabury could be a common prostitute.

"I'm surprised you live in a boarding-house," Amanda said. "According to Myerson's story, the Guardian has a kind of makeshift quarters on the train itself . . . half a boxcar closed in and outfitted as a room. Is that accurate?"

"That's accurate," I said. "But that car is not placed in the train except for long runs. Most of the runs on the Gullytown Line are day runs, between here and St. Louis. No need for sleeping quarters on those trips."

"Well! I'm slightly disappointed, I admit. I find the idea of the Guardian living in a hidden room aboard a train to be rather . . .

romantic, I suppose. Adventurous."

"It's not a particularly romantic job, Amanda. The room in the boxcar is rough, unpainted. Splinters on the walls. It's either hot and stuffy or cold and drafty, never comfortable except on particularly pleasant days in spring and autumn. The room was a sort of afterthought, really, something Colonel Crane dreamed up as a kind of bonus for me after I signed on with his railroad. In retrospect, I think I would have preferred cash."

I turned as I spoke, and suddenly my head swam. Reaching up, I touched the tender, throbbing place on the back of my head where Little Alvin had clouted me with that board. The mere touch of my own fingers caused a jolt of new pain.

Amanda put her hands on my arm and had me sit down on the sofa that stretched across one side of the room. "Lord help us, Dylan, you've got a knot the size of a turkey egg on your head! And he broke the skin, too . . . there's some blood. Dried now, in your hair."

"I don't feel very good, Amanda."

"A blow to the head can do that. I fell off a pony once when I was little. I hit my head on a tree stump while I went down, and knocked myself cold for nearly an hour. And after I woke up I was sick for two days. Just plain, miserable sickness."

"I don't have time for that. I've got to leave on another run on the train tomorrow afternoon. Going into St. Louis. And Colonel Crane will expect me to check in with him come morning. Damn Little Alvin! I hope you *did* kill him when you hit him out there. I hope he's lying dead by the railroad track right now."

"You don't really mean that, Dylan."

"Actually, I think I do."

"No, you're just upset, and hurting. But don't fret. I'll take care of you. I'll fetch some water and a cloth and clean you up a little where he hit you. Then you can rest. Heal up and rest up. You'll feel a world better come morning if you'll take good care of yourself tonight."

Her voice was soothing, her words almost motherly. It made me relax, grow sleepy. Or was that the result of having been hit hard on the head? I recalled times during the war when men had suffered head injuries and great pains had been taken to keep them from succumbing to a resultant strong urge to sleep. Staying awake at such times could be the difference between beginning to recover or slipping into a coma state.

At that moment I didn't care. The need

for sleep was overwhelming, and Amanda's manner was so gentle and calming that I simply wanted to close my eyes and drift away no matter what the long-term result. I heard her talking, worrying about what I'd said about having to leave the next day on the train, wondering who would protect her if I were gone. I was too groggy to reply, but my thought was that she might not need protection, that a woman who could handle Little Alvin the way she had beside the train earlier that night could probably take care of herself. Yet it was also flattering to think that this beautiful young woman wanted me nearby and saw me as a protector.

She rubbed my aching shoulders and talked softly into my ear, though the words were lost on me. Next thing I was aware of, I was in my bed, on my side, head sunk into the feather pillow with its cotton casing cool against my cheek. I saw my clothes in a heap on the floor beside the bed. She'd gotten me down to my underwear and tucked me in like I was a little boy.

Well, this kind of mothering a man could get used to. But I was too staggered to enjoy it the way I might. I lay there with head throbbing, mind filled with resentment of Little Alvin Biggs and heart full of warm affection for Amanda Seabury, along with a thousand questions and some serious worries about just what kind of woman this young beauty really was. Before long I was asleep, though, and all thoughts and questions faded away.

I awakened in the night. Darkness hid the face of the clock on the wall and I had no sense of the hour. When I rolled over, a move that generated a stab of pain through my skull and led me to slowly sit up, I saw that Amanda was on the sofa against the wall, sound asleep.

I hoped Mrs. Finch had no clue about it. She was a deeply moral woman who abided not even "the appearance of evil," to borrow the biblical phrase. Never mind that Amanda was on the couch, untouched, and I was in no shape to be a threat to any woman's virtue at that moment. Mrs. Finch would hold me guilty of evictable offense if she knew I was harboring a woman in my room.

Amanda's exit come morning would have to be carried out cautiously. I'd lose my room if Mrs. Finch caught a glimpse of Amanda's departure.

# 4

I fell asleep again and awakened to daylight through the window. The sofa was empty; Amanda no longer in the room.

I rose, more steady and clearheaded than I might have anticipated, and quickly as I could washed up at the basin, combed my hair and trimmed my whiskers, and dressed. The aroma of Mrs. Finch's cooking breakfast wafted up and teased me downstairs.

The flapjacks were big and butter-drenched, and when drowned in molasses syrup and accompanied by steaming cups of coffee and crunchy bacon, there was nothing finer with which to face a coming day. Mrs. Finch was eating already, alone, when I joined her.

She didn't look at me much, concentrating on her bacon and flapjacks. I did the same for several minutes, then she spoke. "No place in heaven for fornicators, you know."

I looked up at her. "Beg pardon?"

"Perhaps you should. Beg pardon, I mean. Pardon from the Lord."

"What's that supposed to mean, Mrs. Finch?"

"I was just giving you Bible information, Mr. Curry. The Bible says that, you know . . . fornicators will not have a place in the Kingdom of God. Nor drunkards or idolators or liars and such. But it's the first one I think you have to be concerned about most."

Obviously Amanda's presence the previous night had not escaped my landlady's notice. I was sure she was about to toss me out of her rooming house. But I wouldn't go without a fight.

"Mrs. Finch, it isn't what you think," I told her. "I didn't even know that she was in the room. I was asleep. Senseless, actually. I had been attacked by a man . . . see my head? That big knot up there?" I twisted around to let her see the bump where Little Alvin's board had struck me. "I was attacked by a madman over near the train station. He knocked me down with a board . . . I'm lucky he didn't kill me."

"Not lucky," she said. "*Blessed.* Don't give to chance credit that should go to God above. And you are further blessed that

93

Almighty God does not snap the thread of life by which he dangles your soul above the deepest pit of eternal punishment."

The syrup suddenly didn't taste as sweet. "Mrs. Finch, why are you talking to me this way? I told you, there was no wrong done last night. I was hurt and she put me in my bed. And then she lay down on the sofa and fell asleep. I woke up once in the night and saw her there. Then, when I woke up again this morning, she was already gone."

Mrs. Finch frowned at me. "Can I be sure you're telling me the truth, son?"

"I vow before God."

Oddly, this seemed to disturb her. " 'Swear ye not at all,' Mr. Curry. That's Bible. 'Swear ye not at all.' Swear not by heaven, because that is His throne, nor by earth, because that is His footstool."

"Yes ma'am. I know those verses. I grew up in church."

"Well, don't forget the lessons you learned there."

"I'll remember." I began eating faster, ready to get out of there. The first stop would be the hotel, where I hoped I would find Amanda safely ensconced.

I finished my excellent breakfast, took a cup of water and a brush outside and cleaned my teeth. Then it was on to the hotel . . . but along the way I found myself diverted by an unplanned encounter.

Jimmy Walsh was sprawled across an old cracked chair that had sat on the porch of the abandoned Periwinkle Stew Café for the previous three years. His derby hat was cocked back jauntily on his head and he smoked a very fine pipe that I recognized. I'd asked Jimmy about that expensive pipe a year earlier, and Jimmy had told me he'd gotten it off the ground behind the undertaker's place. That's when I'd recognized the pipe. It had belonged to Mayor Spillman, who at the time Jimmy found the pipe was just settling into his grave on Cable Hill, up beside the Baptist Church.

"Still smoking a dead man's pipe, I see," I said as I approached the porch.

Jimmy straightened his derby, sat up, and sent out a big puff of aromatic smoke around the pipe stem. He removed the pipe and studied the stem, which was quite pockmarked by bites inflicted by Jimmy and by Mayor Spillman before him.

"He wasn't a dead man when he smoked this pipe," Jimmy said. "So it ain't like I'm drawing on a pipestem that has corpsey spit all over it."

"I guess not. But the association still comes to mind, you know."

"Anything I can do for you, Dylan? You need me to gather up any information for you?" It was a good question. I'd used Jimmy as an informant several times, and also as an informal street-level investigator. He was good at it . . . Jimmy, in fact, had more natural skill at digging out facts than anybody I'd ever known. Maybe it was because he was so young, and folks didn't expect him to be so perceptive and therefore weren't cautious about what they let him hear.

"I've got a thing or two I'm looking at," I told Jimmy. "Whether I can use your help or not just now, I don't know. If I can, I'll let you know and pay you for what you turn up for me."

Jimmy puffed his pipe and nodded like a tycoon at a company meeting. "Just tell me what you want to know."

"I will, if I decide you can help me."

Jimmy seemed disappointed that I had nothing to hand him right then, but shook it off and changed the subject. "Pretty woman you've been going around with," he said. "I seen you walk to the café with her. I don't know there's ever been a prettier woman in Gullytown."

"You're a bit young to be developing an eye for the ladies, Jimmy."

"Pshaw! Beauty is beauty, like my Uncle John says."

Uncle John was John Byrd, who was raising Jimmy, who was the son of John's late sister. Though it wasn't much of a raising Jimmy was getting. John Byrd kept him fed, kept a roof over his head . . . beyond that, Jimmy was substantially left to raise himself . . . sometimes, I suspected, under abusive conditions. John Byrd beat him, I was nearly sure. Jimmy always denied the beatings, came up with explanations for bruises and scrapes that showed up on him from time to time, and in general declared that his Uncle John was becoming a better and better man by the day, not the common criminal drunkard he'd always been known as around Gullytown.

"Her name is Seabury, ain't it?" Jimmy asked.

"Yes. How'd you come to know that?"

"Uncle John told me."

John Byrd knew her, or at least, knew who she was? That was worrisome news. Why would a lowlife such as John Byrd know Amanda Seabury? "How does he know her?"

"I can't tell you that." But from his cagey manner, I suspected it was more a case of won't than can't.

But I knew how to get it out of him.

"Jimmy, there is something you can help me with after all. And you'll have the answer already at hand."

"All right. I'm ready."

"All I need you to do is be honest with me, and answer what I've already asked you. Tell me how John Byrd knows who Amanda Seabury is, and why you were hesitant to answer."

Jimmy was a boy put on the spot. But this only made me more determined to ferret the truth out of him.

"I don't know what I can say," he said. "I don't think Uncle John wants me saying nothing."

I pulled a coin from my pocket and tossed it up and down, letting Jimmy watch it glint in the morning light.

"I have reason to believe that Amanda Seabury is in danger," I told him. "I've vowed it to myself that I'm going to protect her, and you can help me do that by telling me anything you might know about her."

He struggled visibly with that challenge a moment, then turned to face me squarely.

"Uncle John says that there's some bad things going on with that woman. Serious bad things. He says there's a lot of bad men coming to town because of her."

98

Not a lot of information there, but what there was meshed with what I'd heard from Amanda herself. One would expect bad men to be drawn to town if in fact she was the intended victim of a hired killing, as she claimed.

"Jimmy, your uncle is right," I said. "Amanda Seabury does have bad men after her. One in particular I know about, a fellow named Alvin Biggs, who I used to know in St. Louis. A real maggot of a man. Keep this part between you and me, but he's been hired to kill her."

Jimmy's eyes went so big I could see the whites of them all the way around the irises.

Then his eyes narrowed all at once. "Are you sure about that, Dylan?"

"Reasonably sure. Why do you ask?"

"Just . . . just because."

"Not much of an answer, Jimmy. Why do you have that look on your face? You're not usually so cagey with me."

"I, I think my Uncle John lied to me, Dylan."

I had to laugh. "Does that surprise you, Jimmy? Your uncle isn't exactly the Sunday school teacher type, you know. Just what did he tell you this time that you think is a lie?"

"He said . . . he said that . . ."

And just then, the sound of muffled gunfire from the direction of the hotel drew my attention away from Jimmy, who heard the same as I had and quit talking so fast you'd have thought his throat was cut.

I headed down the street on a run, Jimmy following despite my shouted command that he not do so. By the time I reached the vicinity of the hotel, though, he'd fallen away, or ducked into an alley, or done something otherwise to disappear. Good. I didn't need a boy around to worry about if I was going to have to deal with shooting.

I fished my badge out of a pocket and managed to get it pinned on my chest by the time I reached the hotel. No other law around that I could see, but there were people aplenty, out in the street, mostly facing the hotel with looks of fright on their faces, some of them loping away, putting distance between themselves and whatever had caused the noise.

"Any other deputies, or the marshal, show up yet?" I asked a man.

"No, no, sir," he said, eye on my badge. You're the first."

"Did the shooting come from the hotel?"

"It did, deputy. Third floor, I think."

Good Lord . . . Amanda's floor. Why had

she left the boardinghouse? Why couldn't she have stayed there, in my room, where she would have been safe?

I knew why, and that was what bothered me so. She'd left because I'd made such an issue of how Mrs. Finch would react if she found a woman in my quarters. And merely to spare me the wrath of a pious and prudish old widow, Amanda had left a safe refuge and returned to a place of danger.

Or might there have been more to it than that? I remembered her talk about a need to be on the third floor of the hotel so that prospective "business" clients could find her there. Maybe she'd come back up to the hotel to meet someone.

None of that mattered much. All that mattered was finding out what this shooting was about, and discovering that Amanda was safe. God, I hoped she was!

"Who did the shooting?" I asked the man.

"Don't know," he said. "I didn't see, only heard. I was across the street there, painting some text on a shop window — I'm a sign painter by trade — and that's when I heard it. And a scream, too. A woman screaming."

My legs went numb and threatened to go limp beneath me.

"Has anyone at all, hotel clerk, floor sweeper, random stranger on the street, gone up there to see what happened?" I asked.

"No, sir. I think all of us were waiting for somebody with a badge to do that. Somebody official, like you."

I didn't much blame them. Nobody wanted to walk into the middle of a shooting scrape. And that included those of us with badges pinned to our vests.

But I was the law, even if only a small-town deputy, and it was my duty. So I drew my pistol, said a quick prayer, and headed into the empty hotel lobby in hope that, somehow, I'd bring Amanda out safe and sound at the other end of all this.

Sometimes, in the lawman business, situations spin themselves out quickly, or sometime very slowly. This one went fast.

I'd hardly made it into the lobby before I heard a loud thumping, bumping sound on the staircase. The layout of the place kept me from seeing far up the stairs from the lobby level, so I had to mount the staircase, pistol in hand, and climb in order to find out what was happening.

On the second level, I found out. A man tumbled down the stairs, rolling like a finger-flicked beetle, leaving bloodstains on the stairs as he went. He tumbled out on the landing and stopped, flat on his back, arms out and face staring up with eyes showing a glaze that told me he was dying.

Given his character and habits, it was no surprise to see Little Alvin Biggs coming to such a bad end. But it was not something I'd expected to see happen on this particular night on the second-floor landing of the Gullytown Hotel.

I knelt beside him. His eyes still moved a little, glazed though they were, and it seemed to me that, with some effort, he managed to focus on my face, and his dry lips shaped themselves so he could whisper out my name.

"It's all right, Alvin," I said, feeling sorry for him in the way a man feels sorrow even for a biting dog that dies beneath the wheels of a crushing wagon. "You'd best not try to talk. But tell me who did this."

The lips moved again, but his voice was nearly gone. Just no strength left in him to get it out. "Calvert," he managed to say. He tried for more but couldn't manage it.

Calvert. Good Lord, surely he didn't mean . . .

I heard more bumping around up on the third floor. There was nothing I could do for poor Alvin, so I gave him a kindly pat

103

on the shoulder, rose, and headed up the stairs.

The first thing I looked for when I reached the third floor was Amanda's door, making sure it was closed. God willing, she was safely in there, maybe scared half to death, but not hurt. Yet I couldn't imagine that Little Alvin's showing up here was not related to her presence in this hotel.

Her door was closed, I was glad to see, but my eye was drawn quickly to a man who slumped back in the shadows against the wall at the end of the hall. He was seated on the floor, leaning back in the hallway corner, looking back down the hall at me. It was Ves Calvert. I'd run across Calvert twice before, once during the war, when he was burning the houses of good Confederate folk on the border, and once after, two counties over, when he'd shot down a fourteen-year-old boy who kicked a stray dog Calvert had taken a liking to. Calvert got away with that somehow . . . never arrested, never punished. Rumor was he was proud of that killing, memorializing it by calling himself "Kid Killer," a title with two levels of meaning.

Last I'd heard of Calvert, he'd been in St. Louis, involved in some kind of criminal activity or another. In fact, as I mulled it, I thought maybe I'd heard he was running a ring of prostitutes somewhere.

Along with a chill that ran down my spine, earlier words from Amanda came to me: "For now," she had said, "I need to be at the hotel. On the third floor specifically. That's where I've told my prospective business associates they could find me."

It was an ugly thought. Amanda Seabury, practicing prostitution in St. Louis, perhaps under the pandering thumb of Ves Calvert. Because of her beauty, Amanda would no doubt be quite successful at that foul old trade. Make old Calvert a lot of money.

But what if she left that trade? Or decided to strike out on her own? What if she'd left St. Louis, set herself up in a small-town hotel, put the word out among her frequent "business associates" as to where she could be found? An act like that would generate much ill will on Calvert's part. Enough that he might put out word that he'd pay for her death.

So maybe *that* was the truth behind her story of being marked for death. Maybe it wasn't a husband or former husband who wanted her dead after all. Maybe it was Calvert . . . or had been. I say "had been" because I could see even from where I was at the other end of the hall that Calvert was stone dead. The bullet hole in his forehead was as visible as the dark blood trail that ran down from it across the bridge of his nose.

I walked down the hall, hearing the hollow echo of my bootsoles on the hardwood floor, my eyes fixed on that hideous hole in the middle of Calvert's forehead. Calvert's eyes looked right back into mine, but his eyes would never see again.

Only once before had I encountered a situation in which two men had fatally shot each other at the same time. That had happened on a skirmish field, two bushwhacker bands going at one another.

I knelt and looked into Calvert's dead eyes. "Calvert," I said, "you've got my sympathy for the bad luck that has befallen you here. Little Alvin Biggs probably never hit anything he aimed at in his life before today. I can't say I thought much of the way you lived your life, but I have to pity any man who dies with a bullet through his brain. Sorry it had to come to this for you. But you know how it is: live by the gun, die by the gun."

I'd probably never have been brash enough to say such things to Calvert's face if he'd still been alive and with a working gun hand. But he was dead and gone, the world was better for it, and from him I had nothing to fear.

I went to Amanda's door and lifted my hand to knock. Then I had a mental image of her cowering in there, terrified by all the shooting and maybe aiming a gun of her own at the door. So before I knocked, I stepped to the side in hope of missing any bullets that might come through the door in answer to my knocks.

There were no bullets. Nor was there any immediate answer. Maybe she wasn't in there. Or maybe . . . no. No. I couldn't think that.

I heard a loud groan, but it wasn't Amanda's voice or even a woman's voice at all. It was Alvin, one floor down. I heard another groan, and to my surprise, a calling of my name, barely understandable. He'd gathered up enough strength to call to me.

I was torn. Burst open Amanda's door and see if she was safe inside, or respond to Alvin?

I opted for the latter, reflexively, when Alvin rasped out my name again. Maybe he'd be able to let me know what had happened in this hallway, and how Amanda fit into the situation, if he knew. I'd have only this chance to talk to him, because he'd be gone before long, last-moment rally or no.

His glazing eyes had already told that story.

When I reached the second-floor landing, three people were already with Alvin: two women and a man. The man had apparently come out of one of the rooms; I had the impression one of the women was the man's wife. The second woman did cleaning for the hotel. I'd seen her many times before and knew her name was Mary.

"Mr. Curry!" Mary said when I got there. She seemed glad someone with a badge had shown up. "This man has been shot."

"I know. The man who shot him is dead one floor up. Shot through the head."

Mary gasped and put her hand over her mouth, eyes tearing up. "My God! Is there much mess I'll have to clean up?"

"There'll be some blood and such, I'm afraid."

Mary got up, crying, and ran down to the lobby. I had the feeling she might become sick.

Alvin was still alive and looking at me again. Though clearly in a bad way, he was going through that inexplicable and momentary rallying that is sometimes part of the process of dying.

"Alvin," I asked, "was it you who shot Ves Calvert?" I knew it had to be him, but for the sake of the record needed to hear it from his own lips.

Alvin found strength to nod, and even to lift his left hand and point shakily at the center of his forehead.

"Deputy, do you need us to stay here with you?" said the male onlooker behind me, sounding shaky. "If not, I'd like to get my wife back to our room and away from all this."

"Go ahead," I said. And they were quickly gone, locking themselves inside their room.

"Alvin, can you talk to me at all?" I asked. He nodded and made a noise.

"Did you come to this hotel to kill Amanda Seabury?"

Alvin's deadening eyes narrowed and he shook his head.

"You're lying to me, Alvin."

He shook his head again.

"Then why did you come here?"

He closed his eyes and almost seemed to be sleeping. I feared he was dying at that moment, but the eyes opened weakly and he whispered something I couldn't quite hear.

"What, Alvin? Say it again."

"Saint . . . saint . . ." He lost his wind and faded out, eyes fluttering nearly shut again.

"St. Louis?" I said, taking a guess.

He nodded.

"What about St. Louis, Alvin?"

"Pipe . . . pipeline."

"What else?"

"Killing . . . job. Gullytown. I needed . . . needed the work."

And then he closed his eyes and did not open them again. His breathing became shallower, shallower . . . then a wrench and sucked-in breath, and it stopped.

Little Alvin Biggs was gone.

I stared down at his face a few moments, not able to make myself believe he was dead so suddenly. Surely in a moment there would be a sudden inrush of breath, a return of color to the face, the eyes and lips moving again.

It didn't happen. His lips went pallid, his face even more so, and his eyes became marbles under lids that fluttered not at all.

I noticed a scrap of paper sticking out of his vest pocket, and on it a few words scratched crudely in pencil. Curious, I pulled it out and looked it over. It was torn, half the words on it missing. But the ones that remained intrigued me.

It was simply the name of the hotel and the number of Amanda's room. Nothing more.

To my mind, the note lent credence to what Amanda had told me. Someone had told, written, or wired information to Alvin regarding where to find her. I had to believe that Alvin, and probably Calvert, had come to the hotel for the purpose of finding and killing her. His denial meant nothing.

I rose and headed back up the stairs and down the third-floor hall to the body of Calvert. I didn't have to search him long to find what I was looking for. It was a similar note, but this one wasn't torn, so all the words were there. In addition to what I'd already read on Alvin's note, this one also contained a range of dates . . . a two-week span that bracketed the current date.

Whoever had sent these communiqués had let two bad men know not only where but precisely when Amanda could be found in the Gullytown Hotel, assuming that the torn-off part of Alvin's note had contained the same dates as Calvert's. Whoever wrote the notes had to know Amanda well enough to know that her "business," whatever it was, would have her in this hotel at this place and time.

This was serious indeed. Amanda was in authentic danger. As best I could interpret what had happened here, two men intent on carrying out the "killing job" that had been advertised through the "St. Louis pipeline" in the criminal world of that city had chanced to come to her hotel at the same time. Encountering one another and both realizing the other was a competitor for the ugly work at hand, guns had come out and each had killed the other.

I went to Amanda's door and rapped on it. There was no answer. I rapped more, longer and louder. Still no response.

Worried, I forced the door, managing to pop open the latch without damaging the frame and works. Not at all sure what I would find, I entered, looking for her.

# 5

Marshal Henry Myers was small of stature yet commanding of presence, so he seemed bigger than he really was as he leaned back in his chair with his feet propped on his desktop. It was two hours after the death of Alvin Biggs, who was by then a possession of the county coroner and resident of the local undertaking parlor.

"So the young woman is safe?" he said, prompting me along in my recounting of what had happened.

"She's alive. I don't know that she's safe. After Alvin Biggs breathed his last and I figured out what was going on, I went to her room, forced open the door when she didn't answer my knocks, and found she'd vacated the place through the window. Out onto the porch roof, around the far side of the hotel, and down that old rose trellis that stands there. She'd already gone back to my rooming house, sneaked in, and was waiting for me when I got back to my room. That was about an hour ago."

Myers chuckled and winked. "A beautiful woman, waiting for you in your room . . . sounds like you're living the good life, Dylan!"

"It wasn't what you're implying . . . nothing like that. She came to me, I believe, because she sees me as a potential protector. With two men shooting each other to death in her hotel, it was only natural she wanted to get away from there. And only natural that she would seek out maybe the only person she knows in this town."

"She's returned to her hotel room now?"

"Yes, against my advice. Back on the third floor. The shooting incident scared her, but she calmed down and said she had to get back to the hotel because that's where certain people would be looking for her. And her possessions are still there . . . luggage and clothes and such."

"It looks to me like the 'certain people' looking for her are trying to kill her. Are there others looking for her, too?"

"I don't know. She's a mystery. I wish I could figure her out."

"I'm surprised you're not at the hotel guarding her."

"She wouldn't have it. She said my presence there would interfere with what she had to do. Whatever that is."

"I hate to say this, Dylan, but I have to suspect prostitution."

"I've had the same thought, sorry to say."

"Dylan, in the time you've been around her, has she ever behaved in any way that might make you think she might be plying that trade?"

"Not specifically, no. What are you saying, Henry? That the only possible reason she might share company with me is that she sees me as a potential customer?"

"No, no. Nothing like that, my friend."

"I'm relieved."

Myers was in a question-slinging mood. "What was that Biggs said to you at the end?"

"St. Louis pipeline. Killing job. Gullytown."

"What's this pipeline?"

"Criminal lingo. Slang talk among the criminal element in St. Louis. It refers to an informal 'pipeline' of mostly word-of-mouth information that passes through that level of society. It's a way that messages are sent in the criminal world there. And of course, 'killing job, Gullytown' speaks for itself. But Alvin denied that he'd come to the hotel to kill her."

Myers laughed. "What of that? The man was a worm, and no doubt a liar. But what was the immediate motive for them shooting each other? Did those two have a prior history?"

"They did. Alvin, rubbish that he was, was a detective in St. Louis for years, remember. He was involved in some investigations that landed various people in prison, including Calvert one time. Alvin Biggs had enemies, Ves Calvert among them. My guess is that all it took was for him and Alvin to see each other in the same hallway for the guns to come out. Especially considering that they'd obviously come to the hotel to do the same killing job. Neither one would appreciate competition."

"This is a foul business, Dylan . . . bad men coming to our little town for the purpose of killing a woman. Unless there is something here we're missing."

"I've been going over and over it again in my head to see if there *is* a missing piece," I replied. "I even checked with the hotel clerk to be sure that neither Alvin nor Calvert had taken out a room on that floor, just to see if there was some chance they'd gone up there just because that was where they were staying. But neither one had a room on that floor or any other in the hotel. And they hadn't gone up there to see anyone else but Amanda, because she was the only person staying on the third floor. The clerk said she insisted on the third floor when she checked in."

"It's odd that a woman who knows she's the target of killers would advertise her location, even for business reasons, whatever they might be."

"It is."

"And we're probably going to have to question her, get some straight answers out of her. Even if it involves questions we don't want to ask and she doesn't want to answer. And we're going to have to keep her guarded even if she doesn't want us to."

"I agree. But I've got a problem in that regard, at least in the short run. I'm supposed to be on the train today. We're making a run to St. Louis. And I saw Punkin Jones aboard on the last run, which is a bad sign. He gay cats for the Jones gang, you know." I'd fallen into some criminal world lingo of my own there, a "gay cat" being a slang name for one who scouts for a criminal gang.

"I got some news for you, Dylan," Myers said. "You won't be making that run to St. Louis today."

"Henry, when I signed on as deputy, we

agreed that there would be times I'd have to be out of town when you might rather have all your deputies here. My work on the railroad has to come first for me." Hard words for me to say right then, because I much preferred to remain in Gullytown, watching over Amanda, rather than to go riding away on Col. Josiah Crane's railroad, even for only a day or so.

Myers was ready for me. "Yes, that was what we agreed. But you're misunderstanding me. The reason you won't be making the trip today is that the train isn't making the run. I heard that straight from Colonel Crane himself. I ran into him over near the station. He told me there'd be no run today . . . there's trouble of some kind with the boiler. They're working on it today instead of running the train. According to the Colonel, the boiler would never hold out all the way to St. Louis."

The news wasn't a complete surprise. I'd heard talk for two weeks among the train crew that the boiler was developing a problem.

Myers leaned back, lit his first cigar of the day, and made another examination of the notes I'd taken from the bodies of Calvert and Biggs. He squinted hard through the thick clouds of acrid smoke. He smoked cigars as cheap and bitter as the ones I used . . . the kind of cigars you found in bar-top jars in barrel-bottom saloons. Smokes for the common rabble.

"There's something about these notes that intrigues me, but it's something I'm missing, somehow. I can't put my finger on it."

"I know. I've had a similar feeling since I looked at them. Here, let me see one of them."

He handed me the one Calvert had possessed. I studied it, trying to hear what something in the back of my mind was telling me to notice. It continued to escape me.

We talked a little longer, the marshal and I, then went separate ways, he to make rounds, I to head to the hotel and see that Amanda was well. Lord, I hoped no other "business associates" had showed up on that third floor. I had to get her out of there, and if possible, into Mrs. Finch's boardinghouse where I could more easily keep watch over her.

I walked down the street, around a corner, and stepped up onto a boardwalk. The day was pleasant, the street busy. Through an open door I watched a blacksmith at work at his forge. A preacher sat on the porch of his church, books across his lap, a pad of paper on one knee for notes. Down the street the local dress and fabric shop was open and busy, and the hardware store was crowded. Gullytown was no great commercial center, but that day it was a thriving, healthy place.

I passed a sign shop and glanced through the door. Victoria Beech, who ran the place with her crippled husband, was busily painting on a shingle that would soon hang over some new lawyer's office. I paused long enough to admire her artistry, for her lettering work was known across town for its precision and beauty.

And just then it hit me. I knew what Henry Myers and I had failed to detect about those notes. And I wondered how both of us could have failed to figure it out.

Turning, I ran back the way I'd come, hoping to find Myers. Before long, I did. He was walking along, talking with my young friend Jimmy Walsh, who this time was without his pipe.

I loped up to them from behind. Both turned at once, and I gave Jimmy a quick and perfunctory nod, then to Myers I said, "I figured it out. It's the handwriting. Think about it."

He froze like a block of ice, face twisted in concentration. Jimmy Walsh looked up at me. "What are you-uns talking about?"

"Later, Jimmy. Henry, do *you* know what I'm talking about?"

His face changed, realization rising. "Good God, Dylan! It's a woman's handwriting!"

"Yes. We should have noticed it right away. But it didn't strike me until I saw Victoria Beech painting a sign in her shop. That made me think about how women write differently than men, and it came to me that the notes had not been written by a male hand."

"Dylan, is that Amanda Seabury's script on those notes?"

I thought hard. "I don't know for sure, Henry. I saw her take notes when we rode together on the train, but usually her pad was turned up so I couldn't see the writing much. But it could be hers. I don't want it to be, but it could be."

"If it is, Dylan, it puts a whole new twist on a lot of things. Reverses things completely."

Jimmy, feeling left out of a conversation taking place above his head both literally and metaphorically, looked disgusted, muttered a cuss word or two, and wandered off to the alley. It was just as well. I preferred to talk this out with Henry without benefit of an audience.

"We've misjudged this thing badly," Myers

said. "Biggs and Calvert didn't go up to that hotel room to kill Amanda Seabury. They went up there in hopes of being hired by her to kill someone else."

"Who?"

"I don't know. But we'll have to find out. I'm not going to have solicitation for murder done right here in my town, Dylan. Not right under my nose."

I nodded, heartsick. What kind of woman was Amanda, really? I could hardly go two minutes without thinking of her and my infatuation grew each time I saw her. But in my perceptions so far she had been a victim, someone oppressed and endangered by a wicked man. Now, if Henry and I were thinking rightly, it was Amanda who was the victimizer rather than the victim.

"I think she's looking for someone to murder her former husband," I said. "I think it was Amanda herself who put the word out through the St. Louis pipeline that there was a 'killing job' to be found in Gullytown. A killing job to be *found* here, as opposed to *done* here, as we first interpreted it. She spread the word about it through the pipeline, picked herself a location in advance to meet gunnies who wanted to do the job, and went there."

"The third floor of the Gullytown Hotel,"

Myers said.

"Right. That's why she was so determined to be there at certain times. She had to be present for her 'prospective business associates' to find her."

"She's been seeking hired killers," Myers said.

"I think so." The more I thought about it, the worse I felt. I didn't want the Amanda Seabury who was coming into focus in my mind, a wicked and conniving woman, to be the real one. I hadn't liked the notion of hired killers being after Amanda, but I liked *her* better when that had been my perception.

"What happens now, Henry?"

"We've got to have some words with her. If we verify that she is indeed trying to have her husband, or anyone else, killed, then she must be arrested."

"Maybe we're wrong, Henry. Maybe Amanda isn't the one who wrote the notes. Maybe she is in fact the intended victim, like we first believed. Just because the handwriting looks like a woman's, it doesn't mean *she* has to be the woman who wrote the notes."

"We'll not figure it out sitting here, Dylan. It's time to go pay her a visit."

I dreaded it. How could I confront her

with such an accusation? Yet I couldn't deny the logic of the scenario. If Amanda had behind her an ugly divorce and a man who had come to hate her, perhaps she hated him in turn. Hated him enough to see him killed and to advertise the job.

I remembered her conversation with me on the train when she first came into Gullytown. Her seeming obsession with the outlaw Morgan Kirk. And my realization that, initially at least, her interest in me seemed to stem from her erroneous belief that I could lead her to Kirk.

Why did she want to meet Kirk? Maybe it wasn't at all for the journalistic reasons she claimed. Maybe he was her preferred vendor of death, her top choice for delivering fatal punishment to her former spouse.

I could almost have wished I hadn't shared my realization with Henry Myers. I could have kept it to myself. But, no, not really. I didn't have it in me to stand by while murder was afoot.

Our walk to the Gullytown Hotel took an eternity . . . an eternity that ended far too quickly. We entered the big front entrance, Marshal Myers and I, and walked around to the base of the stairs. It took me back to my most recent visit to that same staircase, and the unusual experience of finding the corpses of two men who had managed to kill each other at virtually the same moment.

Some of Alvin's blood remained where he had lain. I stepped over it and headed on up the stairs, Myers at my side.

I left the knocking to the marshal. He rapped, waited. No answer from inside. He rapped again. Still nothing.

The look he gave me was full of worry. My feelings exactly.

"Step back," I said to Myers. I forced the door again, as I had earlier.

"I'm sorry, Amanda," I said as we entered. "But when you didn't answer, I thought the only way was to force our way . . . in." I cut off, looking around.

There had been no need to speak. Amanda was not there to hear me. As before, the room was empty, the window again having provided her a way of exit. One of the curtains even now was sticking outside the window, dragged out by her exit.

Myers and I searched the room. Her possessions were gone. She'd taken her things with her.

In one corner stood a basket to hold rubbish. It was substantially empty except for some wadded paper. Paper of light, buff yellow, similar to that from the notepad Amanda had written on when she interviewed me on that train ride into Gullytown. Odd, how long ago that recent event seemed now.

Myers had his head stuck inside the wardrobe for some reason, so he didn't see me when I fetched the papers out of the rubbish basket. Quietly I smoothed and folded them, hoping I would find her handwriting upon them. But they were blank except for some sort of liquid stain. I sniffed the paper. Coffee. She'd spilled coffee on those pages and thrown them away. No handwriting there to compare to the notes I'd found on the bodies of Calvert and Biggs. I threw the papers back into the rubbish basket.

Myers pulled his head out of the wardrobe. He looked at me, grinning almost like he was drunk.

"Women are wonderful, Dylan!" he said. "The way they look, move . . . the way they smell!"

"What's got into you, Henry?"

"Put your head in that wardrobe, Dylan. It has her smell in it. Some kind of rosewater or perfume or such she wears . . . there's traces of it still in the air from her clothes having been in there. Sweeter than a rose garden. It's enough to make a man weak in the knees."

"Get hold of yourself, Henry," I said, amused at him. Henry, like me, was a bachelor, and often lonely. He had no prospective lovers, to my knowledge, so he probably seldom had the chance to enjoy the perfumed scent of a woman.

"I'm a fool, Dylan. A fool. Fool for the ladies, anyway."

"What man isn't? Where do you think she's gone, Henry?"

"No way to know standing here. We'll just have to keep our eyes open and look out for her."

"I'm going to the train station."

"Why? The train isn't making its run today."

"I've not been told that officially, so it's my duty to show up. And she may show up there, besides."

"You're an exemplary employee for the Colonel, my friend."

"Colonel Crane has been good to me."

Before I left the room, I did go over and take a whiff of the interior of the wardrobe, silly though I felt doing it. Myers was right: the light and lingering scent inside the wardrobe was intoxicating. It made Amanda seem present in the room. And I wished she

127

were, because then I could know she was alive and well.

I checked with the clerk as we left the hotel. Amanda Seabury had checked herself out.

Was she leaving town? Not likely. No train today, if Myers was right. And the stagecoach line had closed down months before, driven out of business by the railroad. So if she'd left town, she'd done so by some private means.

The other alternative was that she wasn't leaving town at all, but simply shifting her residence away from the hotel. Maybe she had gone to the boardinghouse to seek lodging.

It was an exciting thought. I liked the idea of Amanda as a neighbor. Never mind my questions about her character. Suspicion was one thing, proof another. I had no unquestionable indicator that she was anything other than what she said she was, no real direct evidence she was testing potential hired murderers. There were two notes written in feminine handwriting. Or were they? Maybe they'd been written by a man who happened to have a feminine flourish in his penmanship.

I decided right then to think the best of Amanda Seabury until I had some absolutely solid reason not to do so.

Myers was right about the train schedule for the day. I knew it as soon as I reached the station and saw the locomotive side-tracked and half disassembled, a huge piece of block-and-tackle rigging looming over and around it, holding up heavy masses of black locomotive machinery. Workers moved about on and in the locomotive, bravely oblivious, it seemed, to the metal hanging above them on rigging that to me looked insufficient to hold it.

Old Otto was there, pacing slowly up and down the platform, looking restless. Otto despised alterations of schedule and loathed delays in particular. He'd spend his day fuming and pacing, and probably give Colonel Crane himself a lecturing the next time he saw him. I went to Otto and began small-talking with him. Sure enough, he was keyed up over the delay.

I threw in mention of the fact that the delay allowed the train to be made safer, something that in the long term mattered more than a momentary inconvenience for passengers who might want to travel to St. Louis that day. Otto, with his innate drive to protect and serve passengers, could not argue with that. He slowed his pacing.

"Try not to be too frustrated at being stuck here, Otto."

He sighed. "You are a fortunate man, Dylan, You have two lines of work, and on days such as this can divert yourself through work with the town marshal's office."

"If you want some sort of work on the side, Otto, you could probably find clerking work over at the mercantile or feed store. Something you could come in and do on days like this."

"If I were younger, sir, I'd do it. But I'm not what I once was. The notion of taking on something new isn't one I can handle."

"Otto, have you by chance seen the pretty young woman I was sitting near on the train about the time we had the trouble with the man stumbling and falling on that woman?"

"Seen her today, you mean? Well, yes, I think I did."

"Where?"

"Right over there, walking on that board-walk. A gentleman with her."

"A gentleman? Did you recognize him?"

"No. He was a tall fellow, broad face, ruddy. Hair dark and going to gray. Very straight way of walking. Serious expression on his face. And a kind of mark on his face. Over near his left ear, just a kind of big mole or dark streak, like this." Otto rubbed his finger downward directly in front of his ear.

"I'll be!" I said softly.

"Do you know someone like that?"

"I've known somebody like that in the past. I hope the man you saw isn't the one I knew."

"Bad man?"

"Bad. But the man he works for is worse. If he still works for him."

"I do hope that the young lady is safe and well," Otto said. "She's so lovely! And she reminds me of a woman I knew once, many years ago, in Baltimore. A woman I will never forget."

This might be a story worth hearing. Some other time, though. "You're an old romantic, Otto."

"You can't know the half of it, Dylan, for it would be a tale too passionate for a man to share within the bounds of conversational decency."

I headed for the boardinghouse, not to go home, but to see if Amanda was there. I found Mrs. Finch and made up a story about thinking I had seen a light burning in the window of a room that had been empty. Was there a new boarder in the house?

Well, there was one inquirer, she said. A young woman, quite appealing. But Mrs.

Finch had not been free to talk to her . . . things were boiling over on the stove and a disaster was brewing in the kitchen. So the woman, and the tall man with her, had gone off with talk of a later return. Mrs. Finch had seen them, ten minutes later, driving down the street in a familiar buggy, the rental unit from the local livery. The big man had been driving, with a horse, probably the one he'd ridden in on, tied to the back of the wagon and trailing along. They'd headed west. As for why I'd seen a light burning, Mrs. Finch couldn't account for that. I borrowed her key and promised to check the room to make sure all was well.

Because of what Otto had said, I asked if Mrs. Finch had noticed a mark on the man's face. Yes, she said. A dark mark down the side of his face, like a mole. At first glance she'd thought it had been whiskers, until he got close enough to her in the light to let her see it was apparently a blemish or birthmark.

Bad news. It sounded more and more like the mystery man now with Amanda could very well be who I suspected he was. Mrs. Finch quizzed me how I knew the man with the young woman had a distinctive mark. I evaded answering.

Depressing! I couldn't help but be drawn

to Amanda, but more and more I saw aspects of her manner and behavior that were troubling. I wasn't sure I'd ever truly get to know who this woman was.

I'd never been much of a drinking man, had seen too many lives ruined by the stuff to want to take much part in it, but that evening, after a delicious supper at Mrs. Finch's table, I headed across town toward the Indian Princess House of Refreshment, a local saloon. With me went Ben "Sugar" Kenzie, a local widower who often visited Mrs. Finch. I'd noticed that he usually came around at times when he was likely to catch her putting a meal on the table. He never failed to receive an invitation to dine, nor failed to accept it.

I'd asked him a time or two about his interest in Mrs. Finch, a woman I could never picture marrying again, as devoted as she seemed to be to the memory of her beloved late husband. Loneliness, though, could drive people to look for new happiness, new loves. In her case, I'd believe it when I saw it.

Sugar Kenzie and I took a roundabout path to the Indian Princess, Sugar being wise enough to know that he'd never stand any kind of chance with Mrs. Finch if she knew he visited saloons even a little. She was fiercely strict on alcohol. And plenty of other things.

We entered the saloon through the back and found a table. Lots of folks in the place that night, lots of bustling about among the saloon girls. The badge on my chest drew a few dark glances, but I didn't feel particularly unwelcome. The Indian Princess wasn't known as a haven for lawbreakers and toughs as some other saloons were. And that, maybe, is why I wasn't as prepared as I might have been for what was about to happen.

# 6

The Indian Princess was known around town for one thing in particular: it always had ice on hand, brought in by the Gully-town line on a car with thick double walls stuffed in between with sawdust. A drinker at the Princess could get ice in his whiskey or gin, or enjoy that rarity on the frontier: beer that was *cold*. Beer chilled in an ice-filled tub. That was what had drawn me there that night, and I took care to sip mine slowly, wanting it to last. Sugar wasn't so inclined. He slurped down huge swallows so that his first glass of beer was empty before I'd gotten mine reduced by half.

Sugar was finishing his second beer by the time mine was gone. And though he had a typical old-man kind of pride in his ability to handle his alcohol, the truth was he was already getting a little bleary and slurred. He didn't drink much as a habit because of the risk of being caught by Mrs. Finch, moral watchdog of Gullytown, and the alcohol affected him far more than he realized.

"So, Sugar, are you going to get around to marrying Mrs. Finch one of these days?"

"Marrying!" he almost came out of his seat. "Why would a free old bird like me get into a cage? Huh? Tell me that, Dylan Curry!"

I shrugged. "You could do worse than Mrs. Finch, you know. She's a fine woman."

"But how would she be atop the old feather tick, huh?"

"Good Lord, Sugar, I've never even thought of something like that as . . . as *possible* with Mrs. Finch! I always figured there must be a reason she and her late husband never had children."

"Hell, boy, her kind are sticks of dynamite, I tell you! Don't let that mouse exterior fool you!"

Now, this was getting interesting. "Dynamite, huh? You know that from experience, Sugar?"

"Not with *her.* But I've been around. I got an eye. I know dynamite when I see it."

As homely as Sugar was, my first thought was that his "women friends" probably required a few coins to make the dynamite explode, so to speak. I found myself hoping

136

he wouldn't marry Mrs. Finch. I liked Sugar, but she deserved better.

I was ready to signal the barkeep for another round of beers when a loud, glassine crash from behind the bar startled me. I turned to see what had happened, in time to see a big section of mirror fall to pieces and clatter to the floor. The barkeep lithely jumped over the bar and headed for a man who stood at a table, his chair lying on the floor behind him, apparently overturned by the speed and vigor with which he'd risen.

"What the devil?" I said.

"That man threw a whiskey glass into the mirror," said Sugar, who was seated at an angle that had allowed him to see it. "He appears to be mad about something."

"Barkeep's pretty mad too, now," I said, rising.

"Why you getting up?"

"I'm deputized in this town. If there's trouble it's my job to react."

"You're paying for that mirror!" the barkeep shouted at the glass-throwing drunk. "That mirror ain't going to come out of *my* pay!"

The drunk yelled something that didn't seem to be real words, and swung his fist. A bad move. The barkeep was not only stone sober, but athletic, and ducked the swing with the grace of an ancient Greek Olympian. Lunging at the same time, he came up against the drunk with his shoulder slamming him just under the armpit. The drunk grunted as the wind was driven from his lungs. Spittle flew and he went down, crashing across an adjacent table where five men had been playing cards. Chips, cards, and the dregs of five whiskey glasses erupted volcanically and went in all directions.

I was almost to the scene of the action when a familiar and welcome voice bellowed from the doorway. I turned to see Henry Myers darkening the doorway, his big Remington pistol in his right hand. He was too small a man to be physically intimidating, but possessed the ability to scowl like Beelzebub with a case of piles, and the dark gleam of his eye added a foot to his height and fifty pounds to his frame. People moved away from him and his Remington as he advanced into the saloon and through the crowd.

"What the hell is going on here?" Myers hollered, startling a saloon girl who stumbled to one side and bumped a heavy beer mug off a table. It hit the floor heavily, breaking a shot glass that happened to be lying there. The pop of the shattered glass sounded like a muted gunshot and drew everyone's attention, including the barkeep and his drunken sparring partner.

The drunk, whom I recognized as a local lowlife named Dewey Wheeler, spotting Myers and defensively stammered out something that referred to watered-down whiskey. The barkeep threw the drunk into a headlock and looked at the town marshal. "What was poured into that glass was the pure, straight stuff!" he declared. "I didn't water it down! If it was watered down, it was because Dewey himself let ice melt in it. Then he gets mad because the melted ice made it weaker, so he throws his glass into the mirror yonder. Smashed it to splinters!"

"Did you ask for ice in your whiskey, Dewey?" Myers demanded of the restrained drunkard. "I've seen you in here before, and you always take your whiskey with ice. Now I for one think it's mighty good of this here saloon to go to the trouble of hauling in ice just so them who like their drinks cold can have them that way. And if you let your ice melt in your whiskey, it sure as hell ain't the fault of this saloon, and you got no cause to go damaging the property over it."

Dewey Wheeler's choking reply could not be interpreted by human ears. Myers grabbed Dewey by the collar and shoved the muzzle of his Remington up under

139

Dewey's left ear. Now that Myers had the best of Dewey, the barkeep let him go.

But Dewey gave a quick pull and got himself free from the marshal's grasp. He lunged away, making for the door.

I bolted toward him, dodging around the same saloon girl who had caused the beer mug to fall.

I gripped the drunk's shoulder, fingers digging in like claws. Dewey hollered and tried to get free, but I wouldn't release him. "Hold still!" I hollered in his ear.

"Who . . . who are you?" Dewey asked, still struggling.

"He's the Guardian, Dewey!" somebody in the saloon shouted.

"He's my *deputy,* is who he is!" Henry Myers bellowed, moving in and shoving the Remington's muzzle under Dewey's ear again.

And just then Dewey performed a big twist of his body, lifting his feet at the same time so that his weight pulled straight down. I lost grip on the drunk, who landed lithely, twisted again, and came up, now with a knife in his hand. He slashed it across Myers's arm, causing the Remington to fall with a loud clunk to the floor. It was cocked and only by luck or providence did it not go off.

Dewey made for the door, still danger-ously flashing his knife about. I went after him. Dewey might have made it had not a cowboy seated at the last table before the exit put a foot out at just the right time. Dewey went down facefirst, but managed to avoid falling on his knife. Instead he stabbed the tip of it into the floor, and, in trying to wrench it out again, snapped the blade in half. No tip now, just a flat broken edge.

Angered that the worm had gotten the best of me, I slammed my foot down on the back of Dewey's leg, just behind the knee. I dug in hard, pinching the soft flesh of the leg joint between the ball of his foot and jamming Dewey's kneecap into the floor.

Somebody laughed. Somebody else taunted Dewey. Another cheered me and made reference to the Guardian. I kept my weight on Dewey's leg, not willing to let him have a chance at getting free.

Myers recovered the dropped Remington and carried it over to where Dewey writhed like a pinned-down bug. "I'll take care of him from here, Dylan," he said.

Just then Dewey pushed up on the heels of his hands, shifting his body weight and turning just enough to throw me off bal-ance for a moment. Dewey managed to free himself from the crushing weight against the back of his knee, and came up with the broken knife in his hand.

He wheeled and faced me. Myers, surprised by the speed with which it all happened, fumbled and dropped his pistol again. Dewey, one of those types who is oddly at his best when intoxicated, deftly kicked it under one of the nearby tables, where it was retrieved and hidden by a saloon patron who had a history of problems with the local law, and no inclination to lend a hand to Myers or me.

I grabbed Dewey by the collar, but it tore and Dewey was free again. He turned and thrust the broken knife at me.

I winced and grunted as the stubbed blade cut through my shirt and into flesh. Dewey pulled it out, stabbed again, again. I groaned, lost footing and fell backward. The back of my head slammed hard against the edge of a table. A head already sore and injured by the blow that Alvin Biggs had inflicted on me. I passed out, cold and senseless at that moment as a dead man.

# 7

When I came around again, I knew where I was within half a minute. I saw the familiar walls of my room in the Finch boarding-house, but I didn't know how I'd gotten there, who had brought me, or how long ago it had happened.

I hurt. Midsection. Sharp pains, but with a dull radiating misery that spread throughout my torso. I shifted in my bed, winced, felt a throb at the back of my head, and a sense of fullness. Reaching back carefully to feel the back of my head, I found a folded cloth bandage, tied in place by soft cloth strips around my forehead and neck.

What the devil? Something had happened to me, but I couldn't remember what. I was injured, bandaged, hurting here and there, and back in my room when the last place I could remember being was . . . was . . .

It came back. The saloon, the drunken Dewey, the struggle, the broken knife . . .

the stabbing. My fall. The flashing view of a familiar but unexpected and unwelcome face. My head striking the side of a table . . . then nothing.

Then this. Somebody had carried me up there, bandaged me, put me to bed. I sat up carefully, conscious of my wounds, and looked around for clues.

I found none. I got up and tried my legs. I was weak and slightly dizzy, and moving around made my head hurt worse. But it felt good to stretch my muscles and stand upright like a man should. The need for bladder relief became overwhelming, though, and I made use of the chamber pot hidden under the bed.

I paced the room and went to the window-paned door that led out onto the porch, where I had spent many idle hours with a cigar and a book, watching the people of Gullytown pass below me. Those times for me were not wasted. I'd found that the more I simply watched people, the sharper an observer I became, the more focused a thinker and analyzer of human behavior, and therefore the better at my work.

I settled in the rocking chair on the porch, shifting until my wounds hurt a little less. Slowly I began to rock, looking out over the street, which was lit by the dimming glow of a Missouri sunset.

*Sunset?*

I was confused. I stopped rocking, pondering. It had already been night, well past sunset, when I'd gotten involved in the ruckus in the saloon. Full dark when I last remembered being aware of anything before that moment. And yet it was obvious that another day had passed since then, another night coming on. Or was it just one night? How long had I been laid up in that room, anyway?

I pondered and rocked again, even more slowly, staring out over the railing and only half-seeing what lay beyond it. Next thing I knew, I was opening my eyes and it was even darker. I'd dozed in the chair. I blinked into the night sky, focused on the moon, and wondered again what day it was, how I'd gotten there, and how badly hurt I'd been.

I heard noise from the room behind me, rose and went back inside. Someone was at the door, rattling a key in the lock. I went to the door and opened it before my visitor had a chance to finish the job. The door swung open to reveal Mrs. Finch. She stepped backward as the door opened, obviously surprised to see me.

"Mr. Curry!" she declared. "You're awake!"

"I am indeed." My voice was quite scratchy as if unused for a long stretch . . . another indicator that I'd been laid up there for more than just a while.

"Are you all right?"

I cleared my throat. "I seem to recall being stabbed. And falling and hitting my head."

"Yes, that's the story I was told by Marshal Myers when he brought you here two nights back. You should stay away from drinking establishments, young man. That's the kind of places where such bad things occur."

"Two nights! Did you say two nights?"

"Yes — this is Thursday, that was Tuesday."

I'd been lying in that bed, apparently, for two nights and two days. It was hard to believe.

"Perhaps you shouldn't be standing just yet, Mr. Curry," Mrs. Finch said. "We wouldn't want you to grow dizzy and fall, or to reopen your wounds."

I did not feel I was going to fall, but to appease her motherly concerns I went back and sat down on the bed. I touched my wounded midsection tenderly.

"Are you hurting?"

"Not bad. Just aware of the wounds."

"The marshal told me that the knife that

stabbed you had a broken blade, which made it short. That was good, in a way, because it wasn't long enough to do much damage inside you, the doctor told us. But it made some ugly cuts, and you've bruised quite badly around the wounds."

"Have you been caring for me, Mrs. Finch?"

"I have. I hope you don't mind it. Someone had to see to you, and since you are in my rooming-house, and I'm just an old widow who has the time, it seemed sensible that I watch over you."

"I deeply appreciate it, ma'am. I'm sorry you had to bear that burden alone."

"Oh, I've had help. You've been visited a good deal, Mr. Curry. The marshal has come, and Sugar Kenzie, and some of the folks from the railroad, including Col. Josiah Crane himself. And that lovely young woman who has now taken a room here — Miss Seabury. All seemed very concerned about you."

"Amanda, Miss Seabury, has taken a room here?"

"She has. One floor down, first up from the stairs."

"Did she tell you how long she would stay?"

"No. But you know I don't demand any

147

promise beyond a month. It makes my little boardinghouse here more useful to people. When they need to stay just for a short term, well, I can take them in where other places that want long commitments can't, or won't. And for those who stay only a short time, there's always somebody ready to take their place when they go."

"You are a wise woman of business, Mrs. Finch."

"Thank you, Dylan. Now, may I ask you a question?"

"Surely."

"How well do you know Miss Seabury?"

I wondered what was behind that question.

"I can't say I know her well. I met her only when she came into town on the train. I've talked with her some, dined with her."

"There was a shooting death, wasn't there? In the hotel, outside her door?"

"There were two. Two men fired at each other at the same time, and each hit the other."

"How terrible! But they weren't local men, were they?"

"They were not. One was a fellow from St. Louis whom I knew when I worked there. He was a detective by trade. Not a very good one, not a good man, for that matter."

"Do you think he went to heaven when he died?"

Typical kind of question for Mrs. Finch. "I . . . rather doubt he did."

"His life was a tragedy, then."

"Indeed it was. He was a pure waste of flesh and bone, that man."

"Who was the other man?"

"Fellow named Ves Calvert. A Unionist bushwhacker during the war, and afterward a lowlife who ran a whoring establishment . . ." Remembering who I was speaking to, I paused and coughed a few times as a distraction, hoping she'd not heard me clearly. I rechose my words. "He ran a business of ill repute in St. Louis. He was no better a man than Alvin Biggs. Probably worse. He hated Alvin because Alvin, before he hit bottom, helped put him in prison for a time. So when the two of them saw each other in the hotel, it was probably inevitable that shooting would break out."

"Why would such men go to the hotel at the same time, here in our little town? Why would they even be here? Gullytown does not have a history of attracting criminals."

"You are right, Mrs. Finch. I can't account for it."

"So this Calvert was a man who operated

a sinful business?"

"He did, yes."

"Why would such a man come to visit Miss Seabury at her hotel?"

"I don't know, ma'am."

She shook her head, the image of offended righteousness. I knew what she was thinking. Same thing I was.

"Mrs. Finch, I can't say I know certainly what the nature of Amanda's business was in the hotel, but I don't think it was . . . what you're thinking."

"I hope not. I do not want a soiled dove inhabiting one of my rooms. Mercy! What if she tried to use my own dwelling as a place to practice such an evil trade?"

I wouldn't say it to Mrs. Finch, but my suspicions about Amanda were more severe than hers. Mrs. Finch suspected her of prostitution. I suspected her of soliciting for murder. I hoped she was guilty of neither.

"You're bound to be starved, Mr. Curry," Mrs. Finch said. "I did manage to stir you half awake and get some broth and soup into you a couple of times, but that was all the nourishment you've had."

"Yes, I am hungry."

"Supper is cooking right now. I'll bring a tray up to you as soon as it is ready."

I sniffed the air. "Chicken?"

"Yes. Fried. Potatoes, gravy, biscuits, beans."

"Sounds like paradise, Mrs. Finch. Absolute paradise!"

She blushed and looked away. "You're too kind, Mr. Curry. You're just like my poor late George — he loved my fried chicken so much! When he talked about the cooking I used to do for him, he would say the very thing you just said — 'paradise.' He was a man who truly appreciated his wife, and loved the food I prepared for him."

"He was a good man, I'm sure, and certainly fortunate to have a fine wife. I'm sorry I didn't have the chance to meet him. And sorry that you're without him now."

"Oh, after fifteen years alone you grow accustomed to it. But I still miss him dearly." She paused, wistful. "About this time every day I used to make him a pot of coffee. Would you like some with your meal?"

"Yes, thank you. You're a wonderful woman, Mrs. Finch."

"Thank you, Mr. Curry."

A voice from the doorway interrupted the conversation. "Mrs. Finch, might I come in?" asked Amanda Seabury, who had quietly come up the stairs while the landlady talked to me. She was standing in the

151

doorway to the room, her entrance having gone unnoticed by either Mrs. Finch or me.

"Amanda!" I said, suddenly more conscious of my disheveled appearance. I brushed at my hair with my fingers. "How are you?"

"The question is, how are *you*?" she replied.

"I'm awake, and seem to be doing well enough. Mrs. Finch has been good to me, and she tells me you came by to see me earlier."

"I did," Amanda said. "I heard you were hurt, so I came to see how you were."

"I must get back to my cooking," said Mrs. Finch, looking at Amanda with distrust. She headed for the door, and Amanda stepped inside to give her room to pass. Amanda's posture and manner reflected tension I couldn't account for.

"I can't believe I slept for two full days," I said. "I suppose it must have been the blow to my head when I hit that table."

"Partly, yes. And partly, it was this." Amanda reached into her bag and pulled out a small, brown medicinal bottle, half full of liquid. She held it up for me to see. "I gave you some of this, to make sure you slept," she said. "I'd heard you had been stabbed, and was afraid you'd stir around on your bed and get your wounds opened up. So I poured some of this between your lips and you swallowed it. Laudanum tastes like the devil's tea, but it helps you sleep and eases pain."

"I guess I should thank you, then."

"Perhaps not. The doctor certainly didn't thank me. He came up to check you while I was here, and saw what I had done. He told me he considered it dangerous to give you a strong drug that soon after you hurt your head. He said that a 'cracked skull and an opiate should never be mixed.' It made me feel bad that I'd done it. But please know that I did it out of good intention, believing you needed rest to recover. I began to worry very much, though, when you didn't wake up for so long. That's why I've come up here today . . . to make sure you were still alive."

"Well, alive I am, as you can see, so all's well. I'm sure I did rest more soundly thanks to your medicine." I gently touched my injured skull. "Good Lord, I'm beginning to feel like one of those bags that pugilists hit to strengthen themselves . . . I had two blows to the head — one from falling on that table in the saloon, and one before that from being clouted by Little Alvin there beside the train. No wonder I have such a headache!"

153

"Is it making it hurt more for you to talk?"

"I don't think so. As long as it's just talk. But I don't think I could comfortably shout just now."

"I hope to not give you reason to shout. But I was almost ready to shout myself out in the hallway just now. I almost didn't even come in."

"Why?"

"I was out there longer than you and Mrs. Finch may have realized. I heard you talking . . . and I heard some of what was said. Mrs. Finch, I take it, thinks I might be a . . . 'soiled dove,' as she called it . . . a prostitute, a harlot? Someone who will sully the high moral quality of her rooming house?"

"Amanda, I'm sorry you heard such a hurtful thing."

"I also heard your defense of me, if you could call it that. Very little outrage in your voice, it seemed to me."

"Amanda . . . again, I don't know what to say. Mrs. Finch is a fine woman, and my landlord . . ."

"Mine as well. But I do not like taking insult even from a 'fine woman.' "

She left me wordless a few moments. But the whole thing was kicking my mind back into full steam again, cutting through some of the murk left by two days of sleep en-

154

hanced by a tincture of opium and alcohol. It seemed to me that this might be a good time to find some answers about Amanda Seabury.

"Amanda, I understand your offense. But consider it from the point of view of people who don't really know you. You declared yourself in need of being in the hotel, on a particular floor and in a particular room, for the purpose of 'business' that you didn't specify. That alone would rouse questions, and reasonably so."

"Oh, so any woman who comes into a new town for business is adjudged to be a harlot, and that, you believe, is 'reasonable?' "

"There's more to it than that, Amanda. You must consider that two men died outside your hotel room. Gunned each other down. And one of those men proved to be a man known in St. Louis for operating a prostitution business."

"Which has nothing to do with me."

Her outrage was to be expected, I guessed, but she was actually making me a little angry. Why should a woman who had seemingly deliberately built an aura of mystery about herself be surprised when others found her mysterious and tried to figure her out?

So I laid matters out clearly. "Amanda,

listen to me. I personally found notes on the bodies of both Alvin Biggs and Ves Calvert — Calvert being the one with the links to ill-reputed business in St. Louis — and those notes both referred to your particular hotel room, and had references to a 'killing job.' "

She lifted her brows. "Then clearly those men had come to the hotel for the purpose of killing me. Instead they killed each other when they recognized each other."

"Amanda, maybe that's why they came to your room. But I can't lie: it's hard to believe that now. Because of the notes."

"What do you mean?"

"Those notes were written by a woman's hand. Which can only lead me to wonder if maybe Biggs and Calvert came to your room not to do a killing job then and there, but to be hired for a killing job to be done later, and elsewhere. The note could be read either way."

She looked at me with evident shock. "Dylan, are you saying that you suspect me of trying to hire out a killing?"

How could I reply? She was exactly on target. But I couldn't make myself acknowledge it to her face. I merely stuttered out something meaningless, then fell silent.

Tears came to her eyes. "So I suppose it

will require me being murdered before you'll believe what I've told you!"

"Amanda, I don't expect you to like what I'm saying. All I can ask of you is to try to understand how those kinds of suspicions might arise."

"I cannot, *will* not, 'understand' such a thing! How could anyone think such things of me?"

"Because people don't really know you. I myself don't really know you! And you can't tell what somebody is by simple appearance."

"So I *look* like a prostitute or somebody who would try to hire a killer?"

"Like I said, I don't think that there's really a particular 'look' that goes with those things."

She paused. I decided to see what I might be able to prompt out of her. "Amanda, just to try to make things seem clearer all around, let me go back and continue what I was saying before. You came into town, followed by a foul fellow like Alvin Biggs. You talk about business you were to conduct in a hotel room and say that Biggs and maybe others were under hire by your former husband to have you killed. Then Biggs and Calvert kill each other off in the hallway outside your room, and both of them carry notes, written by a woman, telling them to come to your room in regard to a 'killing job.' And on top of that, you came to town obsessed with finding Morgan Kirk, supposedly for journalistic reasons . . . yet Kirk is an outlaw who has recently developed a reputation for taking on hired killing jobs. It just all fits together in a way to rouse questions and uncertainty."

Mrs. Finch showed up with food and coffee, then retreated downstairs again. For a few minutes the food kept Amanda and me distracted from our previous uncomfortable conversation. But only briefly.

"Amanda, tell me something. I'm told you were seen in the company of a man with a birthmark on his temple. From the description, I'd guess that man to be Leonard Spradlin. Is that true?"

"Leonard who?"

"Spradlin. Was that who it was?"

"I don't know any Leonard Spradlin. I've never even heard the name."

Now, that was hard to believe. If she really was a journalist with an interest in the lore of outlaws, particularly the outlaw Morgan Kirk, it seemed impossible she would not know of Leonard Spradlin, his longtime associate. "There was a man, someone you were on a wagon or buggy with. Mrs. Finch saw you, and saw a birthmark on the side of the man's face."

"Oh! Mr. Talbott! Yes. He's a man I was talking to about perhaps buying a horse and buggy."

"You're in the market for a horse and buggy?"

"Maybe. I find myself thinking that this town could use a good weekly newspaper. I might want to stay here and create one."

"We've already got a newspaper."

"But not a good one. And I know you agree with me about that. I heard you call it a 'rag.'

"Well, that's true. And if you can create a paper here that does a good and accurate job, and doesn't focus on me as some kind of great American hero to the point of being embarrassing, I'll support your work very much."

"Thank you."

"But let's get back to this horse-and-buggy man you say you were with, this 'Talbott.' Is he a local fellow? Because I've never heard of a horse trader hereabouts by that name."

"He has a horse-trader lot over near Gryner Hill."

"Uh-huh. Morgan Kirk's home territory."

"Why did you bring Kirk up?"

"Because he is somebody you seem devoted to meeting. And because Kirk's sidekick in crime is a man named Leonard Spradlin, who happens to have a birthmark on the side of his face. And who perfectly matches the description of the man you were seen with, the man you say is Talbott."

"You believe I'm a liar, don't you, Dylan!" Her voice sounded like she might be on the verge of crying.

"Amanda, I don't doubt you because I want to. I'm forced to do it. Please answer me straight-out: did you meet with Leonard Spradlin for the purpose of hiring him to carry out a killing, or to lead you to Morgan Kirk for the purpose of hiring Kirk for a killing? Or for any other purpose you might want to meet Kirk?" Lord, I couldn't believe I'd dared to ask that. Any friendship, or more, that I might have hoped to have with Amanda Seabury was surely now doomed.

She slapped me. That I hadn't expected. It wasn't a particularly hard slap, but given the bad condition of my bruised and abused skull, it felt like the force of . . . of, well, a derailing train.

But it jolted out of me any desire to demur to her. "Fine, Amanda. Hit me if you want. But here's the hard facts: you've claimed that someone, apparently your former husband, has hired out your killing. Yet I've seen no clear evidence of anyone actually trying to kill you. The man you claimed was following you to kill you, Alvin Biggs, did nothing but grope a woman on the train while ignoring you."

"He also came to my hotel with a gun, and used it."

"But not against you. Against another man who had come to the same hotel to visit the same room . . . yours. And both of them carrying notes concerning a killing job, written in a feminine script. Did you write those notes, Amanda?"

"I most certainly did not! My *God*!" She slammed down her cup of coffee, making it splash, and headed for the door before I could think of any way to stop her. She lingered a moment in the doorway, turning to say a firm "Good evening, Mr. Curry!" Then she slammed my door, stomped away, and I heard the door of her own room slam.

Mrs. Finch would have words with her about that. Door slamming was as taboo as drinking and swearing and fornicating in the Finch boardinghouse.

# 8

I visited the office of Colonel Crane the next morning, where I received the surprising news that the anticipated run of the train to St. Louis had not happened yet. I had assumed that it had occurred during the time I was senseless in my room. But the boiler problem had proven more dangerous than had been first thought, and the train had remained sidetracked at the Gullytown station for repairs all throughout my laudanum-enhanced two-day rest. The train would run again very soon, though. The next morning it would pull out at last for St. Louis, and Colonel Crane was glad to see me up and around again, because he wanted me to be on it. Though at times I grew weary of traveling on the train, I was ready for that run. Life had felt strange since I'd last arrived in Gullytown, and breaking the pattern would do me good. And I had a notion in mind of some good I might be able to achieve while in St. Louis.

When I was finished visiting with the Colonel, I took to the streets. Too much time off my feet had left me stiff and a little sore, so I was eager to walk the discomfort out of my muscles. As I walked, my thoughts turned to Amanda and our unpleasant parting the night before. I felt a fool for it. My doubts and questions about her were valid, of that I was sure, but surely I could have managed to broach the matter in a less off-putting way. I was still attracted to the woman, and hoped that at the end of all the questions I'd find that she was not the deceiver she seemed to be. I wanted to like her and respect her, and to receive the same from her in return.

I rounded a corner and stepped up onto a boardwalk. Drawing in a deep breath, I felt a vague sting, a reminder of the stabbing suffered in the saloon brawl. Touching my midsection lightly, I strode carefully, looking around, neared the boardinghouse that was my home and glanced up. What I saw brought me to a halt.

A curtain moved in a second-floor window, but not before I saw the image of the person who had been holding it up, looking out onto the street. It was a face I'd not seen in years, but recognized without question. Leonard Spradlin.

Wait a moment . . . that window . . .

I glanced up again, and sucked in my breath sharply. The curtain was pulled back again, and a figure looked out at me . . . but it was not Spradlin this time. It was Amanda Seabury, and for a moment, only a moment, her eyes met mine. The curtain fell at once and she blocked herself from my view.

Amanda Seabury was at that very moment up in her room in the boardinghouse, and with her was Leonard Spradlin, right-hand man of the infamous Morgan Kirk. Any possible doubt was removed: this man was no horse trader named Talbott. It was Spradlin.

Of course, it was possible that Spradlin had presented himself to her under a false name and Amanda didn't know whom she was actually dealing with. But given the combination of her obsession with finding Morgan Kirk and Spradlin's close association with the same, that possibility seemed overly coincidental.

I headed straight for the boardinghouse door. It was my duty as a marshal's deputy to confront Spradlin. He lacked the notoriety of his more famous partner, but still he was a known and wanted criminal. I could not in good conscience allow him to roam freely in that town if I knew he was there. And on a more personal level, I didn't want him around Amanda. Lord, what if she was telling the truth about being a target for killing? And what if Spradlin was here to do that job? I hurried my pace, entering the rooming house through the back entrance and going straight for the staircase.

I heard the front door slam loudly as I mounted the stairs, then Mrs. Finch's voice, high and protesting. I ran up the stairs to Amanda's door and found it open and her room empty. Where had she gone? Had Spradlin made off with her?

I ran back down the stairs and circled back into the house toward the front room. There I found Amanda profusely apologizing to Mrs. Finch for the rude manner in which "Mr. Talbott" had slammed the door on the way out. He'd been in a hurry, she said, late for a business appointment.

Business appointment? I knew why he'd run. He'd seen me on the street, recognized me, and had known I'd recognized him, too. I'd never really had much direct dealing with Spradlin, but had encountered him during the war years and knew him for who and what he was, just as he surely knew me.

"Where is he?" I demanded of Amanda. "Where was he going?"

"I don't know. He just said he had business to attend to and had to go. Then he ran down the stairs and out the front door."

"Which he *slammed* most loudly," Mrs. Finch threw in as if slamming a door was a crime on the level with murdering the local parson. "I don't think I care much for this Mr. Talbott."

"His name isn't Talbott," I said. "That was Leonard Spradlin."

Mrs. Finch frowned. "Leonard Spradlin . . . the same one who associates with the outlaw Kirk?"

"The same. I saw him looking out of the window as I passed outside, and recognized him right away. I think he knew that I'd spotted him, and that I'd be up looking for him. I think that's why he fled so quickly, and went out a different door than the one he figured I'd use."

Amanda spoke haughtily. "Mrs. Finch, his name is Talbott, and he is a trader in horses. Mr. Curry here is, I'm sure, sincere in what he says, but also mistaken."

Either Amanda was advancing a deliberate deception, or she was honestly persuaded that Spradlin really was named Talbott.

Amanda glared at me. Not even anger could diminish her beauty. As I looked at

166

her, I made a willful choice: I would, for the time being, assume the best regarding her. The doubts I had would inevitably linger, but I would give her the benefit of them.

"Amanda," I said, "I take you at your word. If you say this man is a horse trader named Talbott, then I believe you, at least in this sense: I believe that you are telling the truth *as you perceive it.* I believe that this man has told you that his name is Talbott. But I must assure you that, in fact, he is Leonard Spradlin, a man not to be taken lightly . . . a man who is associated with crime and danger, and whom you should avoid."

Mrs. Finch cocked a brow condescendingly. "You'd best listen to him, young miss! He's the Guardian! The very one you've probably heard of. He was writ up in the *Review* . . . story was all over the country."

"I know who he is," Amanda said in ice-cold tones. She turned and left, heading upstairs toward her room. But she paused a moment, looking toward a massive bookshelf that stood near the base of the stairs.

"Mrs. Finch," she said, "I've been meaning to ask you about that remarkable shelf. What kind of books are those? Bibles?"

"Indeed they are," Mrs. Finch said proudly. "My late husband was a collector of Bibles. The older and bigger and heavier the better. He had the shelf built specially to hold them. The weight of it with all his Bibles inside was so great he had extra bracing placed under the floor where it stands."

"It's a very singular collection, and a beautiful bookcase," Amanda said.

"Thank you," she said. "My George always was so proud of his Bible collection. He was a great believer in the Bible. 'The word of God crushes the head of the wicked,' he always said."

"A Bible verse?" Amanda asked.

"I . . . I don't know," Mrs. Finch said. "I think it was just something George might have come up with to say."

This was all very familiar to me. I'd gone through almost exactly the same conversation when I'd first moved into the rooming house. Mrs. Finch was always pleased and ready to show off her late husband's collection of antique, massive Bibles.

Amanda went upstairs to her room. I braced myself to hear her slam the door, but she closed it softly.

Mrs. Finch shook her head. "I don't know what to think of Miss Seabury," she said. "There is something about her that is . . . puzzling. And you know my earlier-expressed concerns."

"I think both of us should keep our eyes open for the man she was with," I said. "As a deputy of this town as well as in my capacity of seeking to protect the Gullytown Line, it is no insignificant matter to have Leonard Spradlin roaming free in this town. And it is Spradlin I saw, regardless of Miss Seabury's assurances to the contrary."

"I'll let you know if I do see him, I promise you."

"You are a fine citizen, Mrs. Finch."

"I do try."

It was one of those experiences in which something once heard and then forgotten comes rushing back, prompted by a commonplace sight or event.

In this case the commonplace sight was Jimmy Walsh. I actually smelled him before I saw him . . . smelled his cheap pipe tobacco, more precisely. He was still puffing that dead man's pipe of his, and loitering in an alleyway . . . a typical habitat for him.

"Hello, Dylan Curry," he said in that more-grown-up-than-I-really-am voice of his. "What brings you out today?"

I stepped into the shadowy alley, where I went nearly blind for a few moments, my eyes still adjusted to the bright sunlight of the street.

"What brings me out? Do I need a partic- ular reason?"

"Why, hell no, Dylan! I was just talking. Making noise. You know."

"Well, I'm out this morning roaming the streets, looking for annoying little blabbers. You seen any?"

Jimmy was drawing hard on the pipe, the tobacco burning out. He cussed softly and knocked it out of the bowl against the side of the building beside him. "Nah. Not a one."

"Tell me about Leonard Spradlin."

The boy pocketed the cooling empty pipe and stared past me out onto the street. The change in angle of view gave me a clearer look at his face, and I saw something that troubled me.

"Leonard Spradlin," he repeated. "I'm surprised you're asking *me,* Dylan. You'd know more about him than I would. He's from Texas, I think. And he's rode with old Morgan Kirk for many a year. Got a funny kind of big old mole or something on the side of his face, all spread out like icing on a cake. Real gentleman type, particularly with the ladies. But he's trouble, mostly because when you see him around, you know Kirk ain't far away."

"Thanks for the history, Jimmy, but that

170

wasn't what I was looking for. I know Spradlin's story. What I mean is, have you seen or heard that he's in town right now. Right here in Gullytown?"

"Ain't *seen* him, but I heard he was here."

"Who told you?"

Jimmy looked away and was sullen as he answered. "Uncle John."

I had an even better look now at what had disturbed me before. The bruises were terrible. "Jimmy, talk to me. What happened to you? You look like the Indian nation just danced on your face."

"Nothin' happened to me."

"Don't feed me manure and tell me it's apple pie, boy. I got two good eyes, and I can see that the whole side of your face is as blue as a horse breaker's butt. How'd it happen?"

He shrugged, pulled the pipe out of his pocket again, and concentrated inordinately hard on scraping out the inside of the bowl with a fingernail. "Got into a fight with a feller."

"Must have been a big fellow."

"Nah. He was about my age. A little bigger than me."

"What's his name?"

"Hell, I don't know."

"Why'd you fight him?"

"I forget."

"Local boy?"

"I reckon." A shrug.

"I've not seen any local boys your age lately. Don't happen to be many of them in Gullytown. Seems I'd be familiar with him."

"You calling me a liar, Dylan?"

"If the shoe fits, Jimmy. Tell me straight: has your Uncle John been beating on you again?"

He turned his back on me and I expected to see him stomp off down the alley. But he went nowhere. "I reckon I can take care of myself."

"In a fight with another boy, I'm sure you can. But if John Byrd is taking a stick to you, I doubt you can take care of yourself then. I'll not hesitate to deal with him about it if he's hurting you."

"He'd only hurt me worse later if you did that."

"So it is John who hit you?"

"I didn't say that."

I could see that I was going to run him off if I kept pushing. So for the moment I let it go, and brought up the matter that had come flashing back to me when I'd realized it was Jimmy in the alley.

"Jimmy, do you remember when we talked over at the Periwinkle Café? I mentioned to you that a fellow named Alvin Biggs was in town, trailing Amanda Seabury because he was under hire to kill her?"

"I remember. Biggs was one of the two shot dead in the hotel right after that, right?"

"That's right. But what I want to ask you about is something you said that day. You asked me if I was 'sure' that Biggs was after Amanda. Then you said something about believing your uncle had lied to you, and before you could tell me what he lied about, we heard the gunshots from the hotel and couldn't talk anymore."

"Yeah, I remember all that."

"Well, what I was going to ask you that day was what your uncle had lied to you about."

"I was going to say that he'd lied to me about why Miss Seabury came to town. If what you said about her was right, then he had to have lied to me."

"What's John's version?"

Jimmy dug out his tobacco pouch and took his time filling the pipe bowl. He typically weighed his words when talking about his Uncle John, one of several indicators that his relationship with his substitute parent was not good, and probably abusive.

Jimmy got his pipe burning and filled the alleyway with acrid smoke. My patience began to falter, so I asked my question again.

Jimmy shrugged. "He told it all backwards to what you said. You said she had somebody trying to kill her. The way Uncle John told it, it's the other way around. She was trying to hire somebody to do a killing for her. She got word out all around St. Louis about it, and then some there who heard about it spread it more. And she came to Gullytown to meet up with folks who wanted the job."

"Why come to Gullytown for that? Couldn't she just meet her hired killers right there in St. Louis?"

"According to Uncle John, she left St. Louis so she could avoid the person she's trying to get killed, until she could get him dead.

"Maybe your uncle is wrong about this one, Jimmy."

"He might be. There's something odd about him these days. He ain't been himself lately. Something's going on with him. He's all distracted and gloomy."

"Enough to hit you?"

"Maybe."

"He'll hear from me about that."

Jimmy looked forlorn and said nothing.

"Jimmy, do me a favor, and don't repeat that stuff about Amanda hiring a killer. I want to know for sure what the truth is before such a thing spreads further."

He shrugged. "Ain't no call for me to be talking about it with nobody, anyway."

It was time to face head-on my doubts about Amanda Seabury. I headed back to the boardinghouse to find her and see if I couldn't reach some sort of settlement of my uncertainties.

"She's not here," said Mrs. Finch. "She left a while ago, while you were out taking a walk. Took a walk of her own, I think. But not alone."

"Spradlin?"

"No. Not this time. It was that drunkard John Byrd. Which is another cause for me to have concern about her."

As much as I disliked agreeing with a woman who at times was a self-righteous and prudish moralist, I had to do so this time. Especially given what Jimmy Walsh had told me. Indications were that John Byrd, who obviously had had some contact with Amanda already, given all that he'd told Jimmy about her, was in the running to become a hired killer.

"Did she say when she was coming back?"

"She said nothing. Just stomped down the stairs the same angry way she'd stomped up them, breezed past me without so much as a howdy-do, and out the door she was. She walked away, and around the corner yonder, and then she was gone. Not five minutes later, though, I saw her over there, across the street, standing in the shade of that tree and talking to John Byrd."

I had to figure Amanda out, and *what* she was about. If she was in trouble, I would help her and protect her. If she was seeking trouble then I would be true to my duty and stop her.

"I think I'll make a few rounds about the town, Mrs. Finch."

She beamed at me. "I'm so pleased to have a man of the law living here," she said. "The law is ultimately God's voice, I believe."

"All I know is that it's my job to uphold it." I tromped away and headed down the street and around a corner.

"Dylan? Is that you? I was just coming to find you."

I turned. The voice was Amanda's, and it came, softly, from the same dark alley where I'd talked with young Jimmy.

She emerged from the darkness, looking nervously about, then withdrew again, out of sight. "Amanda? What's wrong?"

"I'm . . . I'm afraid to be out here in the open. *He* might see me."

I glanced about. "There's no one here, Amanda, no one but me. The street is empty right now."

"Are you sure?"

Another look around. Far, far up the street, Gullytown's first drunk of the day staggered out of a saloon and stumbled into a watering trough, making a huge splash. He was so far away I couldn't even make out what curse words he was saying as he floundered out again. "Nobody but some drunk way up the street, and he's paying no attention to anything down this way."

She came to the end of the alley and glanced around the corner. She saw the drunkard, squinted to clarify her vision, then relaxed a little. "That's not him," she said. "Thank God . . . maybe I've lost him."

"Has somebody been after you today, Amanda?"

"Yes."

"Talk to me,"

"There was a man who told me he was going to kill me. He said he was being paid to do it." She looked away, eyes brimming. "Damn my husband! The murderer!"

Well, not yet, but it did appear he was trying. "Amanda, I have to go out of town tomorrow. A train run to St. Louis, one that has been delayed while the train has been under repair."

"Oh . . . I was hoping that maybe you'd be in town for a few days. I'd . . . I'd appreciate any . . . *oversight* you might be able to give me."

"Oversight . . . protection?"

"Yes."

I forgot my doubts and questions about her. She was asking me for my personal protection. It was actually touching. As before, I chose to believe in her innocence through an exertion of will.

"I'll protect you, Amanda. But it might mean you'll have to take a train ride tomorrow."

"You mean . . . to St. Louis?"

"I've got to go. It's my work. And if I'm to protect you, you'll have to go as well."

"But St. Louis . . . that's where *he* is!" She paused, pursing her lips, thinking hard. Nearly a minute passed and something in her eyes changed. She nodded. "That is all right. Yes . . . that will be fine. I'll be on that train with you, Dylan."

Suddenly she pulled a watch out of a pocket in her skirt, and looked at it. She very softly whispered something that sounded to me like a curse, then put the watch away, took my hand and all but pulled me down the street.

"Where are we going?"

"Walking. Just walking. When I get scared enough, and tense enough, I have to walk it out, walk it off."

Run was closer to it. I'd never seen a woman achieve such a pace and keep it up so long. I kept up with her, but by the time we reached the edge of town and headed toward a grove growing alongside the little canyon of Gully Creek, I was winded.

"Where we going?" I asked.

She turned and looked at me, and moved to position herself in a particular spot, turned a particular direction . . . or so was the impression she gave me. Just as she opened her mouth to speak a loud pop sounded from the grove, and her skirt gave a sudden jerk, as if someone had tied a string to it and yanked it from behind. I heard the sudden *whup* of the moving fabric as her skirt danced out behind her. When it floated down flat again, there was a hole cleanly punched through it.

I grabbed her and put myself between her and the area from which the shot had come. At the same time I yanked out my pistol and put three shots right through a thinning cloud of gunsmoke that hung at the edge of the grove. I doubted I'd be lucky enough to hit the shootist, but certainly I'd scared him half to death. Maybe driven him off.

"Let's move, Amanda," I said. "Let's get you away from here."

Keeping myself protectively between her and the grove, I led her back to town. No further shots were fired, but I did not feel safe until we were on the street, shielded by buildings and the presence of other people.

We went to the nearest saloon and found a table nearly hidden in a shadowed corner. We sat down, Amanda near tears, trembling and breathing jerkily. I sat down across from her and leaned over the table, spreading myself as much as possible to help her feel shielded. Once hidden from the view of all others, Amanda fell apart. Tears streamed down and her shoulders heaved . . . so did her bosom, though I tried — vainly — to be a gentleman and not notice the latter.

"Well, do you believe me *now*?" she asked. "Do you believe someone is trying to kill me?"

How could I not believe it? I'd seen the bullet rip through her garment. "I do believe you."

"God . . . that bullet tore right through my dress!"

"I know. I saw it."

"I swear, I could feel the heat of it brushing by my leg . . . my limb." She trembled and seemed to wilt down several inches.

"Mrs. Finch isn't around. You may say leg without fear of scandal."

She scooted back, and, under the cover of the table that was between us, gathered up her skirt and did a quick examination of her legs.

"Good God!" she exclaimed. "There's a streak where the bullet passed across my skin!"

"Did it leave a furrow?"

She squinted, concentrating. Shook her head. "No. It didn't cut, just scraped and burned. It's all right if you want to look."

I moved around and did look. She was lucky indeed. A bullet passing close enough to a person to leave a mark on the flesh without breaking it is a rare event. Even a quarter-inch shift in the trajectory would have made a difference.

Just as my eyes were being attracted to less relevant parts of her exposed legs, she put her skirts back down, pulled herself together, and looked squarely at me. "I think you owe me an apology."

"I wasn't looking at anything I shouldn't have."

"That's not what I'm talking about."

"So what should I apologize for? It wasn't me who shot at you. It wasn't even me who walked us out of town just now. It was *you* leading *me* out there."

"You owe me an apology for what you asked me before, about whether I wrote those notes you found on the bodies of the dead men in the hotel. You owe me an apology for doubting my word."

"I . . . I . . . perhaps I do. You're right, Amanda. That shot taken at you just now is strong evidence in my book that you are indeed a target."

"Yes. I'm the target of a killer, not the *employer* of a killer. There's a huge difference there."

"Obviously so. I ask your pardon for my doubts earlier on. But do try to see it from my side, Amanda. All those notes referred to was a killing job, which could be read in two different directions, so to speak. And they were in a woman's handwriting.

"I understand. And I forgive you for misunderstanding."

"Thank you. But there remains a question. If it wasn't you who wrote the notes, who was it?"

"Some other woman, obviously."

"Such as . . ."

"I don't know. Maybe the woman my dear former husband was wooing while we were still married."

"What's her name?"

"Lorena."

"What was her last name?"

"I . . . don't remember. I don't think I ever heard her last name."

"Of course now she's Lorena Seabury."

"What?"

"She's married to your former husband. Right?"

"Seabury is my *maiden* name."

"Oh! I'm sorry. I've assumed all along that you were continuing to use your married name."

"I no longer have the husband, so why should I bear his name? I returned to my maiden name after the divorce."

"Again, just a wrong assumption on my part. Forgive me?"

"I forgive you. Again." She fidgeted. "Are we just going to sit here? Doesn't this place serve beer?"

"You want one?"

"I do."

The beers weren't as cold as those served at the Indian Princess, but just as robust. Amanda was on her second one by the time I ventured to say: "I probably should not have come here. I should have searched the grove where the shooter was hidden."

"But you would have left me alone out there had you done that."

"Yes. Which is why I didn't."

"And whoever fired that shot would have fled from the grove by the time you got there, anyway."

"Probably. Who do you think it was, Amanda?"

"My Lord, how could I know? Whoever took the 'killing job,' I suppose."

It could be anyone. It troubled me to think that any person we passed on the street might be the one who had taken a shot at Amanda and come so close to striking her. I was unnerved.

Yet I was relieved. At least I finally had good reason to take her at her word. That bullet had come too close for me to believe it was anything but an attempt upon her life.

"How long will the St. Louis journey take?" she asked.

"It will be an overnight stay. We'll head back toward Gullytown the next morning."

Once the journey to St. Louis began, old Otto took Amanda under his wing and made her comfortable. At one point she gave him a tiny pecking kiss on the cheek, and he blushed red and beamed like a light-house.

The eastward journey was blessedly un-eventful. I saw nothing to make me believe the train was under threat. No Punkin Jones in the railroad car, no sightings of potential robbers outside on the landscape. The only odd occurrence I encountered was seeing Amanda back around the boxcars as I walked toward the passenger car before the trip began. She was standing close to the cargo door of a particular car. The door was open slightly and Amanda glanced in repeat-edly. Beyond that she seemed to be looking around in general, fearfully, as if to see who was watching her. Only when she noticed me staring at her from among the stream of boarding passengers did she move away from the boxcar and come in my direction. When I asked her what had intrigued her about the boxcar, she seemed unnerved by the question and tried to brush it off. When I pressed the question, feeling intuitively that there was something going on that I should know, she told me she had been considering stowing away on the train rather than riding in the passenger car. The idea of isolation, of secret riding away from the prying eyes of spies and hired killers appealed to her.

But she'd not done it. She sat with me, in a posture that seemed to draw her up within herself, make her small. This was a frightened young woman.

But for the moment she had nothing to fear. The train ran smoothly, its boiler problems repaired by then. Despite Amanda's manner, I found the journey one of the more pleasant ones I'd undertaken in months.

By the time we reached St. Louis, though, Amanda was more tense than ever, studying the faces on the platform before she would disembark. She was the last off the train, descending to the platform as if she expected to be seized right away by her hated former husband or some killer under his hire.

Personally, I was more worried that whoever had taken a shot at her from the grove outside Gullytown might have hidden among the passengers and was now with us in St. Louis. In this city it would be easier to manage a murder than it would in a small place such as Gullytown, where crimes stood out.

"So where will you go while we're here, Amanda?"

"Well, I want to make the visit I've had planned. But most of the time I'd hoped to stay near you."

An appealing prospect . . . but it didn't mesh with what I had to do. "Well . . . there is something I have to take care of while I'm here," I said. "Someone I need to see while I'm in town." I didn't add that once I'd reached that person, there would be questions to ask that I wouldn't want her to hear.

"Someone you 'have to see,' " she repeated. "Business? Friendship?"

She was a nosy creature. "Both."

"Male or female?"

I almost laughed. "Why would you care?"

"Ah!" she said, brows lifting. "So it *is* a woman you're going to see! I suspected as much."

She was wrong . . . but I could see nothing to gain in correcting her. I ignored the comment.

"Amanda, unless you have a safe place to go, a place in St. Louis you can be where no one will find you, I want to put you up in a hotel. We'll give you a false name and keep you out of sight."

"No. No, not yet. There is a place I can go."

"Safe?"

"I think so, yes."

"Where?"

"The Bellfield Hospital. North part of town."

"I know the place. Why would you go to a hospital? Are you ailing?"

"There is someone there I want to visit. You're not the only person with a visit to make in St. Louis."

"Not your former husband, I hope."

"Oh, Lord, no! Of course not!"

"Well, is there any chance your former husband might know of this someone you plan to visit, and have someone of his own watching the hospital, figuring you'd make a visit there sometime or another?"

"He does not know of the person I'm going to visit. And I doubt he knows I'm in St. Louis."

I wasn't so confident. If her hidden pursuer in Gullytown had been watching her, he would know she had entered a St. Louis–bound train. A quick wire to her former husband would be all it would take to get that news to St. Louis long before we arrived.

"I'll rent a buggy and we'll ride to Bellfield together, then I can go on to where I need to be. Let's go," I said, eager to get on the move.

# 9

Bellfield Hospital operated in an old building of stone painted a dirty white. I drove Amanda there in a rented buggy with a screeching axle. We arrived with me still ignorant of the identity of the individual she had come to the hospital to visit, and no indication she was inclined to tell me.

"There's no need for you to wait for me," she said. "I need to make this visit alone. You can go about your own business, and I'll be waiting for you when you come back to fetch me."

"I don't know it's a good idea to leave you alone here," I said as she climbed down. "There could be danger here as much as back in Gullytown."

"I'll be fine. Just come back when you're ready." And she was gone, awaiting no response from me.

She entered a door at the end of a long wing laid out in a westward orientation.

Through a bank of windows facing me I saw her walking down a hallway and stopping at a particular door. She paused there, appeared to be calling inside, and entered.

I said a quick mental prayer for her safety and drove the buggy out onto the street and around a corner. I was on my way to a familiar neighborhood where once I had made my living.

I'd found time to wire Mark Hannibal from Gullytown that I was coming, so when I walked through the office door he was not surprised to see me. In fact he had coffee already bubbling on the stove in the same battered pot I remembered from years before. He poured me a cup as I walked through the door. Even the yellow cup was familiar.

Mark Hannibal and I had been the best of friends and probably always would remain close. There'd been a time when Mark nearly became my brother-in-law, but the romance between me and his sister, Jerusha, died too early. Mark had always blamed his sister for the failure of our relationship, but often, in my private and honest moments, I suspected that I was mostly to blame. Didn't matter anymore. Water under the St. Louis bridge.

Mark and I sipped coffee and settled

down for a talk. He made a few joking comments about my growing fame as the Guardian, and laughed loudly. I laughed, too. That was the good thing about Mark Hannibal: he knew me too well to take me as seriously as a stranger might. It felt good to laugh at myself with him. Then we got past the joking and I told him why I'd come.

"Amanda Seabury," Mark repeated after I'd gotten out my story. He frowned in thought and leaned across his desk, chin in one hand, forefinger of the other hand tapping on his temple as he concentrated. At last he leaned back and lifted both hands, palms up, as if in surrender.

"Never heard of her," he said. "Sorry. It's a memorable enough name, and if she is as beautiful as you say, I'd probably be aware of her if ever I'd run across her."

"Are you *sure* you don't know her?" I asked. "I've had the impression she'd be fairly well known around St. Louis."

"*Compadre,* I can't know everyone in this city. Though sometimes I think I know most. She is probably just someone I've not happened to meet or hear of."

"Oh well. Tell me this, then. What do you know about anyone named Brannigan?"

"Brannigan . . . Brannigan." He was tapping his temple again. "I know two Brannigans, know about them, anyway. You talking about Jonathan Perry Brannigan, or Benjamin?"

"Probably the first. I've heard him referred to as J.P. Who is the other one, though?"

"Well-off fellow with a big house on the river. Made his fortune with a stagecoach line before the railroads took over. Kept his fortune by investing his money in railroads."

"And the other Brannigan?"

"Also quite wealthy . . . inherited wealth in his case. His father was a publishing magnate in New York. The son chose to become a practicing journalist. No financial necessity for it, simply a choice of the life he wanted to lead, it appears. He's been quite successful at it. Natural talent and good training. He writes primarily for the *Monthly American Review.* The same magazine that carried the story about you recently, I think."

"That's the one."

"Interesting story. I read it. Did Brannigan write it?"

"No. A man named Myerson."

"I have to wonder what prompted you to ask about J.P. Brannigan, then."

"He is . . . connected to a person of interest to me. What can you tell me about him?"

"Well, I've always heard him described as

arrogant. Vain. Not that he's some classically handsome man with much to be vain about in terms of looks. He's nearing sixty and he's got some girth about him. Beard and mustache, still more dark than gray. The mustache has flourishes on the ends. Curls, you know. The kind of appearance deliberately cultivated to draw attention. For years, until his marriage, he had a reputation as a great romancer of women. Rumor is that his marriage might not have ended his womanizing ways."

"Hmm. Is his wife the kind who might become jealous of, say, a young and beautiful female journalist studying under Brannigan's tutelage?"

Mark's next words nearly knocked the props from beneath me.

"Dylan, his wife *is* a young and beautiful journalist studying under his tutelage. That much I have heard. But I have never seen this young woman, personally, and I do not know her name."

I stared into my coffee. "I'll bet I do."

My mind was racing as I drove the rented buggy back to Bellfield Hospital.

Was the man Amanda described to me merely as a teacher and mentor in fact the same man she had married, the one now seemingly trying to have her killed? If so, why had she taken pains to hide the true nature of her relationship to Brannigan, describing her relationship to him as a professional rather than personal one?

Mark had presented Brannigan as pompous and vain. That notion fit with the image of a man who might be so hurt and embarrassed to be cuckolded by a beautiful young ornament of a wife that he would take extreme action to pay her back.

After the better part of a day spent roaming old haunts in the city and trying but failing to think of much of anything but the mystery that was Amanda, I reached Bellfield and pulled the buggy to a stop at the same spot I'd dropped Amanda off. She was not there. Still inside visiting, maybe. I waited, waited some more. Nurses, doctors and clerical workers left the building, but no Amanda. At last I grew weary of waiting, climbed down, and headed in through the same door Amanda had entered before.

The hospital was dismal, though someone had attempted to brighten the atmosphere through the placement of flowers. The flowers helped some with the bad smells permeating the hallway, but not enough. I walked a short distance down the hall, hoping to spot Amanda. I did not.

I remembered seeing her enter a room. Could I find it? I'd seen her entrance only dimly, through an outer window that aligned with a doorway open into the hall. I traveled the hallway slowly, trying to figure out which door I'd seen her enter.

I entered one room, found it empty. Continued looking.

The next door was slightly ajar, and I had a sense of the room being occupied. I knocked lightly on the door, hoping Amanda would answer.

"Amanda?" I called, softly.

I received an answer. Not Amanda's voice, nor even a coherently spoken word. Just a raspy voice, frail and brittle, making a sound.

I entered the room and found an old woman on a bed. Clearly a resident patient. She was old, but not ancient.

She smiled at me. "Simon, it's a marvel to see you," she said. Her voice sounded a little stronger than before.

I smiled down at her. "Ma'am, I think you've mistaken me for someone else. My name isn't Simon. I don't believe we've met."

She frowned darkly and squinted at me, studying my face. "You're not my Simon?"

Poor woman! Senility setting in. She'd

mistaken me, apparently, for her own son, if I was interpreting the "my Simon" reference correctly.

"I'm not, ma'am. My name is Dylan."

"Pleased to meet you, Mr. Dylan. But are you sure you ain't my Simon?"

"I am, ma'am. Sure, I mean."

She looked sad and seemed older suddenly. With a sigh she sank her head back deep in her pillow. 'Ah, well, I should have known not to expect two miracles in one day."

"Miracles?" I repeated.

"Yes, sir. I had me a miracle today. My daughter came to see me. I ain't seen her since she was a little girl, but she found me somehow, and she came to see me. All grown up and pretty now."

"That's wonderful, ma'am. What is her name?"

"She was always Mandy to me when she was tiny, back before I had to give her up. But she told me she goes by Amanda now."

"Amanda is your daughter?"

"She is. And she's as beautiful as any young lady who ever walked. Prettier even than I was when I was young. And though you wouldn't know it to see me now, I was a great beauty in my day."

I stood there amazed, realizing that this

was Amanda's mother I was speaking to, unless I was to believe that two young women of the same name had visited this woman in a single day. "I believe I know your daughter Amanda, Mrs. Seabury," I said.

She silenced me with a glare. "I don't know no name of 'Seabury.' If you want to know who I am, look yonder on that board by the door. My daughter wrote it down there today as she was leaving."

I looked. Over beside the door was a small, black slateboard, hanging in a frame. On it, written in chalk, was the name OPHELIA KIRK.

Kirk. Amanda's mother, if such this woman actually was, was named *Kirk*!

"Mrs. Kirk, might I ask who your husband is?"

She glared at me and said nothing. Thinking maybe she had not heard, I repeated the question and got the same silent glare in return, intensified.

I moved from that subject and talked with her a while longer, but it was one-sided. My question about her husband had closed a door she would not reopen.

It was a lot to mull over, and it all threw different possible lights onto the mystery of Amanda Seabury . . . or was it actually Amanda Kirk?

■ ■ ■ ■

I had to find her. She was not at the hospital.

The hotel, then. That's where Amanda would be. She'd gotten tired of waiting for me and gone to the hotel on her own. That had to be it.

The Gullytown Line held an agreement with the Imperial Arms Hotel. It was a fine kind of place I'd never consider staying if not for the discount given through that agreement to passengers of the Gullytown Rail Line. As a railroad employee, actually I had it even better than the passengers, enjoying a room rate that was half again off the discounted priced that Gullytown Line passengers paid.

I checked in. The desk clerk knew me from the many past times I'd stayed at this hotel. His name was Daniel, and he made no secret of being proud that he knew me, knew the Guardian himself, knew someone who'd actually been reported about in one of America's most popular magazines. His attitude reminded me of the unwanted admiration I received all too often from the doting local newspaperman Ralph Wiles.

"Need to ask you something, Daniel."

"You just ask it, Mr. Curry. If I know the

answer, by gum, I'll tell it to you."

"Did a young woman take a room here today? Name of Amanda Seabury, though I don't know whether she'd use that name or not. She's auburn-haired, quite, uh, well shaped. Remarkably beautiful face. Maybe the most beautiful woman I've ever met, in fact."

Daniel looked wistful. "Mr. Curry, I wish indeed that she had taken a room here. I see many beautiful women come through here . . . a fair share, anyway. But I don't know I've seen any who would be as pretty as this woman you're describing. If I'd seen such today I'd recall it."

"You would. Believe me."

I took the key and made my way to my own room. It was familiar . . . the Imperial often put me up in that room. I didn't linger long, though. Too restless. Too curious as to what had become of Amanda. Having not found her in the hotel I no longer had any notion of where she would be found. I had personally told her that the hotel she should choose should be that one. Yet she'd not gone there, not yet, anyway. I hoped she was all right.

So I hit the streets, and searched. Mostly a random kind of blind search . . . glancing in café windows, saloons, even dance halls.

No sign of her in those places. I searched until I nearly forgot who I was searching for. I checked other hotels, talked to policemen, and simply looked around. The longer I looked the more tired I grew, and eventually I gave it up as a lost cause. Angry with her for puzzling and worrying me that way, I headed back to the Imperial, realizing as I drew near that very probably I'd find she'd checked in during my absence.

But she hadn't. No one with her name or matching her description had taken a room at the hotel. Disappointed and becoming more seriously concerned about what might have become of her, I went to my room and tried to rest, but ended up back on the street again, searching.

It was long after midnight before I returned. All my efforts had been futile. Amanda Seabury had seemingly vanished into the city of St. Louis.

Tired as I was, it took me a long time to fall asleep.

# 10

Morning brought clouds and the threat of rain, but by the time I'd left the hotel café with breakfast under my belt, the clouds were fading. My worries about Amanda were not. She'd even then not yet showed up. Something had happened, surely. But I had no idea what.

Whatever it was, it couldn't be good. I pictured her being dragged into a carriage by rough men, hauled off and dumped at the feet of her former husband, perhaps alive but just as likely dead.

I should have found a better way to protect her. I should never have left her alone at that hospital. But I had duties to the railroad, duties to Colonel Crane, and to Henry Myers and the law. In making the journey to St. Louis, I'd done what I had to do. And I'd tried to do it in a way that preserved Amanda's safety as much as possible. Seems I failed in that regard, though.

So as I drove the buggy to the station, from which the train would depart within the hour for the return journey to Gullytown, I fought a battle with my conscience. I loathed the idea of leaving St. Louis with Amanda still absent and unaccounted for. But it was my job to protect the train. If something happened to or on the train and I was not present on it as duty required, I would not live easily with myself.

The stable from which I'd rented the buggy stood near the railroad station. I turned in both buggy and horse, took my meager baggage out of the buggy, and headed across toward the train. I hoped that Amanda would show up at any moment and solve my problem. She didn't, but a little boy with tousled hair and an expression of near desperation did. He stomped up to me, forcing me to a halt, and gaped up at me, breathless.

"Are you Mr. Dylan Curry?" he gasped out.

"I am. Who are you?"

"I run errands for the telegraph operator at the station yonder. He told me to find you and make sure you got this." The boy handed me a folded piece of paper.

"Thank you." I opened the paper. The boy lingered. I fished in my pocket and gave him a coin and he darted off.

It was a telegram, wired in from Gully-town. Colonel Crane. Few words, simple message: there was some evidence of possible danger from robbers on the return excursion from St. Louis. No details, no specifics, no identifications of from whom the threat, or the evidence, came. But I knew the Colonel well enough to know his words were to be taken seriously.

That settled any lingering inner debate about whether to stay or go. I had to make the run, had to be the Guardian I was hired to be.

But I still worried about Amanda, and wondered where she had gone . . . or been taken. God in heaven, let her be safe, let her be well.

My hoped-for miracle did not happen. Despite my fervent prayers and wishes, Amanda did not arrive at the last moment to board the train. As it pulled out of the station and began the westward crawl toward central Missouri and Gullytown, I looked back from the rear platform, actually hoping to see her running up to the station, late but not missing. I saw no such thing.

I reread the wire from Colonel Crane, then pocketed it and rose to make a pass through the train, just to see what I might see. I looked for such as Punkin Jones or any other known faces associated with train robbery. Nothing.

I motioned for Otto and he obediently came my way. I led him out onto the passenger car platform for some private talk. Once out there I showed him the wire from Colonel Crane.

"Oh, my!" he said, voice piping. "I wonder what the specific threat is?"

"I'd like to know. The Colonel gave just enough information to keep us on our toes, but not enough to really guide us as to what to expect."

"He probably doesn't know the specifics, Dylan."

"Probably not."

Otto and I rode outside on that rear platform for miles, enjoying the separation from the passengers, the bracing sting of the wind, the freshness of the air. It was easy to grow lulled into a certain bland complacency in such a situation, and this I did, until the clouds covering the sky broke suddenly and the full light of the sun pierced through and stabbed me in the eyes, rousing me.

But the train was making a long, wide turn, and moments later the angle of the train blocked the sun from my eyes again.

The sun shone down from the eastern sky. The train began another wide turn, this one northward, so before long the sun shone on one side of the train and cast the west-facing side in shadow. It also threw a shadow of the moving train itself out across the rolling landscape.

I leaned on the platform rail and looked out to the west. I began to say something to Otto, but cut off quickly, startled by something I'd just seen.

"What is that, Dylan?"

I did not reply, being fully distracted.

"Dylan?"

"Otto, look. See the shadow of the train? Now look closer. Do you see what I do?"

The old fellow squinted and strained that one good eye of his. Then he sucked in his breath suddenly.

"See?" I said. "A shadow. Somebody is atop the train, Otto."

"I see it . . . I see the shadow of him."

"I'm of a mind to see who it is."

"You be careful, Dylan. Given the warning from the Colonel, it could be that whoever is up there is part of a plan to rob this train."

"Just what I was thinking."

"You're going up there?"

205

"I've got to."

"I wish you wouldn't. It could be quite dangerous."

"How else can I see who is up there? It's my job."

"I suppose it is. Don't fall. And for God's sake don't get shot."

"I figure I'm bulletproof, Otto. Remember the last robbery got me shot four times. Surely, after that, fate couldn't be so cruel as to let me get shot again."

He didn't see me coming. The man was seated near the front end of the passenger car, facing forward, coughing some in the smoke and cinder ash that billowed back over the train from the stack up front. He was hunkered down like a fellow who expected to stay put for a time. With his legs dangling over the front end of the car and his hands palms down on either side of him, he was well braced. But he was also not in a good position to get up quickly.

The nearer I got to him the harder it was to remain quiet. I was glad for the noise of the train, and glad that the seated man was looking toward the east rather than the west. If he looked west he would probably spot my shadow just as I had spotted his. But he was obviously transfixed by that eastward landscape. Looking for something, or someone, maybe. Waiting train robbers?

I reached a point about three feet behind him, and he remained as clueless as ever of my presence. The train left its northward route and inclined westward again, leaving behind the mostly flat land we'd been upon most of the way. The terrain grew more rugged, more rocky. The train rumbled more as it progressed.

I tapped with the toe of my boot. It caused the man seated before me to suddenly become aware he wasn't alone, and to scramble to his feet, turning at the same time.

His eyes grew wide as full moons when he saw me there just a yard behind him. Mine did too when I saw who he was. Startled and acting out of reflex, he started to step backward, then realized that would send him stepping into the space between the railroad car we were in and the one before it. He avoided making the fatal step, but lost his balance. He let out a yelp of pure fright, and with face twisting in horror, windmilled his hands as he struggled to keep from falling.

He was about to go over when I reached out and grabbed him by the cloth of the thin jacket he wore. I yanked him back toward me as I stepped farther back onto safer ground.

"Easy, John Byrd," I said. "Don't fall."

Byrd whimpered and fell forward on his knees like a sinner at the mourner's bench. I glared down at him. "John, what are you doing up here on top of this train?"

"I'm just riding, Dylan. I'm just riding, that's all."

"Most folks ride inside trains, not on top of them, John. Unless they're brakemen, which you aren't, or unless they have some reason. Like maybe setting up a railroad robbery."

"I ain't no train robber, Dylan. You know I ain't never done that. I'm up here be-cause . . . uh, because I had no other choice, Dylan. It was the only way I could get a ride back to Gullytown."

"You weren't on the train when it went to St. Louis from Gullytown. I'd have seen you."

"I wasn't in the passenger car. But I was on the train."

"Stowed away, huh? Freight car?"

"Yeah. Yeah, I was."

All at once I remembered what I'd seen before the train left Gullytown . . . Amanda, talking into the open door of a boxcar.

208

Could it have been John Byrd she was talking to?

Mrs. Finch had said she'd seen Amanda talking to John Byrd on the street.

John Byrd was more firmly on his feet now, and turning. But the train gave a jolt and he staggered. I reached out to grab him reflexively and missed him, but he managed to maintain his balance without my help.

"So why didn't you stow away inside a boxcar for the return trip, John? Why ride up here where you can fall off?"

"Uh . . . uh, they had them locked up before I could get a chance. So I had to just climb up here." He looked around the landscape. "Ain't bad, really. I like the breeze and the open sky."

Good Lord . . . his chin was trembling. This man was struggling not to break into tears.

Had it been anyone else I might have felt sorry for him. I kept remembering the bruised face of Jimmy Walsh, though. "Enjoy the open air while you can, John," I said to him, meanly. "You'll be in a jail cell soon enough."

The chin trembled harder. "It don't matter, I reckon. I've been locked up before." A quavering voice.

"Why'd you go to St. Louis at all, John?

You got friends or kin there? Or business?"

John Byrd was in a self-pitying mood. "A man like me ain't got friends, Dylan."

"Business, then."

"I . . . I can't say why I went. Just wanted to go."

"You got friends there, I'll bet. A woman, maybe. Is that it, John? You got you a woman in St. Louis?"

"I ain't got no woman in St. Louis."

"Maybe you don't, but you do have family."

"I got no family in St. Louis."

"I'm not talking about there. I'm talking about Gullytown. You've got Jimmy. He's all that's left of your sister. Yet you treat him bad, John. You beat on him, call him things no boy should have to hear."

John nodded, then looked at his feet. "I know, Dylan. You're right. Anything bad you want to say about me, you're right. And I'm worse even than you know. Because of what I went to St. Louis to do."

"What are you talking about?" I coughed, choked by the smoke from the stack.

"I . . . I . . ." He was having second thoughts about whatever he'd been about to say to me. Maybe he'd just remembered that not only did I work for the railroad, but also for the marshal's office in Gully-town.

The train was still rolling along, and a shift in the wind moved the column of roiling stack smoke off to one side, missing us. The freshening of the air was delicious.

"Keep talking, John. Maybe if you talk up good I'll forget about this little illegal ride of yours when we're back in Gullytown. Maybe I won't even talk to the Colonel about it."

Tears suddenly began to roll down his face. "I'm going to tell you something, Dylan. You know the reason I got up on top of this train today? The *real* reason? I got up on this train to die. So I could throw myself off and rid the world of me. And rid me of myself, if you know what I mean."

"John, I . . . I don't know what to say. All I can do is tell you that killing yourself isn't the way to go. If there's bad things in yourself you want rid of, then kill *those* things. But not yourself."

"I've tried that, Dylan. I've tried to be better. I've tried to put away the liquor and the bad things I do. And it never works, not for long. I always fall back into it again. I want to be a good man, but it seems I wasn't made for that. I'm born to be a worthless old devil, Dylan."

211

"John, maybe you ought not try to go to being a good man all at once, all in one big jump. Maybe you ought to try to be a better man first of all. And just keep going from there. Like taking steps on a journey, or the wheels of this train turning over one turn at a time, over and over."

"So what can I do?"

"Well, you can start by giving me some information right now. Tell me if you know anything about anybody planning to rob this train today."

"What do you mean?"

"The railroad line was given an indication that this train was going to be robbed during this trip to St. Louis and back. No details, just some kind of warning that Colonel Crane knew about. Do you know anything about that, John?"

"Dylan, I've been a bad man, but I ain't never been a train robber. I don't know nothing about this train being robbed."

"Are you sure?"

"I'm sure. I swear."

"All right, then."

"I'm going to throw myself off this train, Dylan. Down there under the wheels so I'll be sure to die. It's all I can do."

"No, John. No. Listen to me: if you want to die, you've got the rest of your life to do

212

it. It doesn't have to be a decision you make right now, right here today. You understand me?"

He sniffled, still weeping, and nodded.

"I want you to try what I talked about a minute ago. Taking a small step to become a better man. Not a perfect man, because you'll never get that far, but a *better* man."

"What can I do Where can I start?"

"A fine place to start is to quit beating a little boy who's never done anything wrong except let himself be born into the wrong family."

He winced as if I'd hit him, and I wondered if I'd been too forthright. "I know, Dylan. It's when I'm drunk that I do it. And I can't help but get drunk. It's like a sickness to me. I got to do it even when I wish I wasn't."

"It *is* a sickness, John. It's one men give themselves by making the wrong choices too many times. It finally gets where you can't make the right one. But it's still your fault, because there was a time early on you could have said no to the whiskey."

"God. God forgive me. I've done nothing but wrong with my life, Dylan. Can I ever change? Really change?"

"I've seen it done. You can change. You can."

"How?"

"I'm no priest or preacher, John. I can't answer all those questions. Maybe you ought to find yourself a good preacher and ask that question to him. Maybe he can tell you the answer. But whatever he tells you, I'm going to bet that one of the first things you'll have to do is be honest with yourself. Face up to things the way they are, not the way you would like to think they are. And I'm going to give you a chance to do that right here. I'm going to ask you to be honest with me and tell me why you stowed away and went to St. Louis."

He winced again. "Do you have some notion of why I did?"

"I've got a suspicion."

"Maybe if you tell me what your suspicion is, I can tell you if you're on the right track."

I knew better, really, than to let a man being questioned start turning the questions around on me and thus taking control of the situation. But some instinct told me that I might get further with John Byrd just now by doing that very thing.

"All right, John. Here's my suspicion: I suspect you were following somebody to St. Louis. A lady. A pretty lady. For a killing job."

He couldn't hold my gaze.

Seeing I was on to something, I laid it out straight. "Was that it, John? Did you go to St. Louis to kill Amanda Seabury and take payment for it from her husband?"

You'd have thought I'd just hit him in the face with a dog turd, the look of shock he gave me.

"No. No! That ain't it at all. Not at *all*! Why would you ask me a question like that?"

"Because somebody is trying to kill Amanda Seabury, John. I know that because I saw her nearly take a bullet outside town the other day. Somebody shot at her from hiding and the bullet tore right through her clothes and nearly hit her. You know anything about that, John? Did you fire that shot? Did you try to kill her?"

I was getting to him. A vein throbbed at his temple. "I can tell you this, Dylan," he said. "You don't know nearly as much as you think. And you sure don't know nothing about picking the right people to trust."

"Explain that to me, John. You're losing me."

"Just saying that things ain't always what they appear to be. People, too. And situations."

"Still clear as a brick wall, John."

"I can't say more than that, Dylan. I can't

tell you things that'll make you lock me up. Wouldn't be prudent of me."

"Is there something like that to be told, if you *were* able?"

He chuckled. "You ain't tricking me, Dylan. You ain't. But you ought to know that somebody has done tricked you."

"Who? And how?"

"I ain't the only stowaway on this train. Didn't know that, did you? There's another who did make it into a boxcar before they locked it up. I was the only one who saw."

It seemed to me John Byrd was trying to change the subject away from Amanda Seabury. Which told me I was getting close to something. "We'll get that stowaway when we get to Gullytown. Thanks for the tip. We'll get him."

He grinned. " 'Him,' " he repeated, then chuckled.

Five seconds passed without words. Then there was no time for more, for the train gave a terrible, shuddering heave and left the tracks. The locomotive rolled out across prairie like a massive iron wagon and tilted right onto its side. The tinder spilled wood and the remaining cars jumped the tracks and went onto their sides.

Next thing I knew, I was in the air, tumbling like a thrown pebble, unable to tell up from down or to see anything clearly except the ground flying up toward me. I slammed it hard, lost my ability to breathe, then rolled over onto my back and looked up to see the heavy wooden door of a boxcar falling down toward me. It had been sent flying up and forward when one of the boxcars behind me splintered and ruptured, and when it descended it chose to do so at the spot I'd come down. It slammed me like a fly being swatted, and all at once I knew nothing at all and had no awareness of anything around me.

# 11

By the time I was part of the world again and worked my way out from beneath the heavy door, thanking heaven all the while that I was able to move, most of the reaction to the derailment was already past. We'd neared Gullytown sufficiently that word of the incident reached the town fast, and Colonel Crane responded quickly by dispatching riders, wagons, and railway handcarts. The Colonel's military background served him well . . . he reacted strategically and logically, not in panic, and set a responsive operation into motion.

I was regretful that things had transpired as they had, with me on the top of the train when the thing derailed. Being thrown off and knocked senseless, then buried in train rubble, left me in no position to be much help. Not that I would necessarily have been better off had I been inside the train. Several passengers were seriously hurt. Five were killed.

Most worrisome to me was the fact that one of the dead was a young woman, so badly mangled that her upper body and face were obliterated. But the color of the dress she wore matched one I'd seen Amanda wear more than once . . . and the rub was that she'd been found in the wreckage of a boxcar. A stowaway, riding without official record of her presence, unknown to the railroad crew.

I tried to argue against the possibility of it being Amanda. But for every argument I found an answer that was uncomfortably plausible. Why would Amanda have stowed away on the return trip when she rode openly in the passenger car on the outgoing journey? *Because something had happened in St. Louis that had forced her into hiding . . . something that probably also accounted for why she had never taken a room in the hotel.*

But in the absence of identification upon the body and any possibility of the ruined face ever being identified, the dead young woman was officially written off for the time being as an unidentified vagrant . . . but Henry Myers was sure that she had to be Amanda Seabury, and told me so. I didn't want to agree with him, but felt I had no choice. What other young woman would have stowed away upon a Gullytown-bound train, particularly one who just happened to be Amanda's build and size?

I didn't want to see the corpse but I had to do it. I persuaded myself it wouldn't bother me too greatly, for I'd seen many a mangled body in the war. But it did bother me. I couldn't get past the idea that the ruined form I was seeing lying there in the undertaker's parlor was the same young woman who had dominated my thoughts for days . . . a young woman who, if circumstances permitted, I might have been able to love.

There were only a few bunches of hair left on what remained of the poor woman's head. But it was hair of a disturbing color. Same color as Amanda's.

After I left the undertaker's parlor I headed out back and was sick in a back alley. Not from having seen mangled flesh, but because I could not doubt that mangled flesh had once been *her*.

There was another mystery related to the derailment, too: what had happened to John Byrd? Like me, he'd been tossed off the top of the train upon the jolt of leaving the tracks. Unlike me, he had not turned up again, either alive or dead. Of course, initially no one looked for him because no one but me knew he had been atop the train. Old Otto, of course, knew there had been *someone* up there, someone I'd climbed up to investigate, but Otto did not know that man's identity. And Otto had been unable to talk, anyway. He'd been knocked cold in the derailment and had drifted in and out of consciousness ever since. All of us who knew him worried for his life, though deep inside I believed he'd pull through. He was a resilient old fellow.

I sat in Colonel Crane's office and smoked one of his good cigars. He was somber but talkative.

"It was no accident, Dylan. I looked at the tracks myself. Found abundant evidence that they were loosened and placed out of line. That train was run off the rails as surely as we're sitting here. And you know that the express safe was opened . . . the express-man forced to open it at gunpoint. Morgan Kirk did this."

"It's farther east than I'd expect to see Morgan Kirk at work, but you're right — his smell is all over this thing," I said. "Of all the train robbers out there, he's the one who has established a pattern of derailment."

"Yes, and it's known he's in Missouri at the moment. He's come home because his old mother is dying over in Gryner Hill."

"That's what they say."

The Colonel rolled his wheelchair out from behind his desk and made a big circle around the room, brows lowered in a frown. A legless man's way of pacing, I suppose. He steamed like a locomotive with a boiler ready to blow.

"Let me ask you something, Dylan, and please take no offense," he said. "I'm asking you because of your association with Marshal Myers."

"Ask away."

"All right. Here you are, men of the law, here for the protection of this town. And a few miles away, there is a known and wanted criminal, an obvious danger to the public, particularly that part of the public traveling upon the railroad. Given that, why have you not simply gone and arrested him?"

"Well, Colonel, it isn't as simple as it would seem," I replied. "Gryner Hill is in a different county, for one thing. Henry Myers, remember, is empowered only as a town marshal here in Gullytown. Through agreement with the county he has the right to make arrests and enforce the law outside the town limits within this county, but in that regard he is no more than a mere deputy of the county sheriff. He doesn't have any authority to cross county lines to make an arrest."

"Ah . . . so my question would be better posed to the sheriff in Gryner County."

"Yes."

"So why does *he* not simply arrest Morgan Kirk?"

"Kirk has years of experience in hiding from the law, and plenty of places that will allow him to be close to his old homestead without actually being on it. There's caves in the hills around there, a whole system of them. I've always heard it said that Kirk and his men know those caves and have hid out in them time and again. And legend has it that much of his loot is buried there. The man has been hiding from the law for more than a decade, Colonel. He's a master at it. And now, because of what happened to his face, he pretty much hides from everyone."

"His face, yes." Colonel Crane shook his head. "I don't find it easy to hold any sympathy for a man who would derail a train and bring about the death of innocent people, and rob my express car besides, but I must admit a certain amount of pity for anyone who is as physically ruined as he is said to be." The Colonel looked down at the place his legs should have been. "Maybe my own experience with disfigurement has overly softened my heart."

"Did anyone actually see Kirk at the scene?" I asked.

"Yes. A little girl She was thrown out of the passenger car when it rolled and tore open. Not hurt, fortunately, but so terrified that she lay where she fell. She told us later that a 'man in a mask' came to her to see if she was all right. When he knelt by her, she was able to see under the mask. She says he had 'a devil's face.' "

"Has to be Kirk, then. 'Devil's face.' Ironic. He used to be known as a very handsome man. Quite popular with the women."

"From what I've heard, Kirk is still a popular man among the people of his own area, ladies and men alike."

"That's right. He's viewed as a hero by many. Like the James brothers. That's another reason nobody has been able to get to him to arrest him. People protect him, hide him in their homes and cellars and such. I remember about three years ago they found out a preacher had let him hide out in his churchhouse for more than a week. A preacher! Protecting a devil like Morgan Kirk. And I believe the sheriff over there is just as protective of him."

"Odd, the kinds of folks people will hold up as heroes."

"War does that, Colonel. But you know that."

"Yes. And in the case of the Gryner County sheriff, a little money slipped under the table doesn't hurt, either."

Jimmy Walsh ate his steak and eggs with such obvious appreciation that I had not the slightest grudge at having spent money on his meal, though I was very nearly broke at that moment. I knew that most of Jimmy's meals were poor ones, corn-bread-and-greens kinds of meals he mostly cooked up on his own for himself and his uncle. A true restaurant meal was seldom part of his life.

On impulse, I had invited the boy to join me for supper at Connor Café, a small but good eatery about three blocks away from the much nicer Palace Restaurant. The Connor was famed in the region for its steak and eggs, and Jimmy admitted that he'd long dreamed of eating those foods in that place, but had never found the money or anyone willing to take him there. Sometimes, he said, he'd sat outside the place in the back alley, just to smell the food cooking. I thought that was a sad tale, and instructive regarding the high cost that comes of a life lived in a liquor bottle. John Byrd had not set out to deprive his nephew by the life he lived, I guess, but that had been the effect. I thought it tragic that a little street boy had been forced to wait so long for a pleasure as simple as a meal in a café.

At that point pretty much everything in Jimmy Walsh's life was tragic. The disappearance of his uncle was no loss in one sense, but it had Jimmy sad and depressed, and I was coming to see that, whatever bad things John Byrd had been to his nephew, he had represented a degree of stability. He wasn't much, but he'd been all that Jimmy had, and I suppose that counted for something.

Not that he was definitely and finally gone. No body had been found, no evidence of him either living or dead. He'd simply disappeared. Maybe he was dead. Maybe just in a saloon somewhere.

"I think Uncle John was doing better lately," Jimmy said, carving off steak. "I think he'd decided maybe he should try not to drink as much. Hell, I saw him looking at a Bible a while back. He can't read, but he was sure astudying the pictures."

I nodded, but in truth I couldn't put much stock in the idea of John Byrd changing his ways, despite all his tears and declarations of repentance while we were riding atop the train. I was too cynical, I suppose. Too familiar with human nature and the fact that it seldom takes turns for the better.

"John was lucky to have you to keep an eye out for him," I said. And it was true. I thought of the many times I'd seen young Jimmy leading his drunken uncle home late at night, or the times he'd come to visit John Byrd in the town jail when he was locked up for fighting while drunk. Jimmy had the patience of a saint and seemed resigned to the role of playing nurse and protector to a man who seemed unable to protect himself.

"Why you saying 'was' lucky?" the boy challenged. "He ain't gone for good. I think maybe he went back to St. Louis."

"How? On foot?"

Jimmy glared at me harshly. He was straining for whatever hope he could find and in no humor to have me snapping the slender threads that held it.

"He'll be back, Jimmy," I said. "When he's ready, he'll be back."

"You said you talked to him on top of the train before it all happened."

"That's right."

"About what?"

"Just . . . things. About how he wanted to become a better man. And he declared he was a far worse man than I could know

227

because of what he'd gone to St. Louis to do."

"What did he say that was?"

"He didn't. It was while we were working around to that that we went off the tracks, and John and I went into the air."

"Did you talk about the pretty lady? Miss Seabury?"

"Yes. She's gone, too, you know."

"I heard she was found killed in the crashed train."

"There was a young woman killed. Amanda's size and hair color, and wearing a similar kind of dress. I'm afraid it probably was her."

Jimmy was eating more slowly now. "I'm awful sorry if she's dead. I don't think she was a good woman, but she sure was a pretty one."

"What do you mean by the 'good woman' part? Do you know something about her?"

"I guess there's no cause to keep quiet about it now. I know she wanted Uncle John to do something bad. I don't know what. But it was something he worried over. He went to her looking for work of some kind . . . that's how he put it to me. 'Looking for paying work.' "

"What kind of work was it?"

"Uncle John didn't tell me much, Dylan.

Not real clear, anyway. But he told me that she wanted to hire him as a shootist. He wouldn't explain beyond that."

A shootist. Did that mean that Amanda was the one hiring out the "killing job" after all?

But what about that bullet that so obviously had been fired at her that day just outside town? How could I account for that?

Maybe it didn't matter now. She was gone, it appeared. It made me heartsick to think of it.

I vowed to myself that Morgan Kirk would pay. Jurisdictions and legalities and practical difficulties of the sort I'd thrown up to Colonel Crane would not impede me. I would go after Kirk as one man pursuing another, whatever it took. I'd see him dead for killing Amanda. Even though I did not know whether he even knew he had done that act. It appeared the motive for the derailment had been to rob the express car. Anyone who got in the way and got hurt, or worse, was probably in Kirk's estimation simply an annoying unplanned casualty.

I bought pie for both Jimmy and me for dessert — apple, fresh and hot — and then a second slice for Jimmy. The boy was in heaven, stomach full of good food, a hot cup of coffee in front of him. When he finished, he pulled out that old dead man's pipe of his and fired up. The boy was utterly shameless about his smoking. I could have scolded him, but to what effect? So I joined him, lighting up a cheap cigar.

"What are you thinking, Dylan?" Jimmy asked abruptly.

"Hmm? Oh, just that I might have to go after Morgan Kirk myself. Avenge what he did to your uncle, and to Amanda and the others who were killed."

"You've met Kirk?"

"I was around him some in the old days. The bad days."

"The war."

"Right."

"Did you ever ride with his band? There's stories out there that the Guardian once rode with Morgan Kirk."

"Those stories are wrong. I never confederated with Kirk. I rode with Jim Parsons' group during the war, not Kirk's. But I did meet Kirk on occasion, but that's all."

Jimmy looked wistful. "Them must have been exciting times."

"They were bad times, boy. Bloody times. Be glad you're young as you are, Jimmy. You don't have to look back and remember all that."

"Sometimes I kind of wish I'd been there.

Just to see it all. Good or bad, it had to be worth seeing."

"It was that. It was that. But it's a shame it had to happen. A fight's bad, even for a good reason. And a family fight is the worst kind."

"Family fight? What are you talking about?"

"The war. Think about it, Jimmy. You'll see what I mean."

"Oh! You don't mean 'family' like me and Uncle John. You mean family like the whole country being a family together."

"That's it. That whole cussed war was one big family fight, people shooting and killing each other who shouldn't have ever come to that."

Jimmy pondered a few moments, and I went back to the last couple of fragments of my pie, laying my smoldering cigar on a dish.

"One thing about the war, though," Jimmy said. "It brought some good things. You got to admit that."

"Like what?"

"Like the slaves getting to go free."

"Yeah, I guess that's right. I never did think slavery was a good thing, even though I fought for the gray and butternut."

"You know, for you, Dylan, there's another

231

good thing the war brought."

"You lost me."

"All the things you went through . . . the fighting, riding around with bushwhackers and border fighters and so on . . . all of that gave you something good."

"Really? What was it?"

"The skill to become the Guardian."

"Well . . . yeah. I guess you're right about that. Though I'd trade it all away if that war could have gone without happening."

Conversation waned. A beautiful young woman and her obviously smitten husband walked past our table, heading for the door. The woman frowned at the stinking cigar butt I'd left on the dish. Jimmy gazed at her so openly it embarrassed me. The boy already appreciated beauty.

"Dylan, I'm sorry for asking this, and I hope you won't despite me for it, but I was wondering if . . ." The boy cut off abruptly and simply stared at Dylan.

"Wondering if what?"

"Well, Miss Amanda was a mighty pretty woman. Beautiful, I guess you could say. The kind of woman that, when you see her, sometimes it's hard to think about, you know, Moses and Abraham and Jesus. She makes you think about . . . other things."

"Even at your age, Jimmy?"

"Yes, sir. Even at my age."

"Well, it will only become more that way as you get a little older."

"I figure so. But here's what I wanted to ask you, and I know it ain't my business, but I know you had some meals with her and such. I been wondering if you and her have ever . . . done what folks do? Married folks."

"Mighty personal question, Jimmy. Not at all proper for you to ask."

"I know. But sometimes you can't help but wonder about things like that. And think about stuff you ain't supposed to. Is it that way for you, too? Or is it just me?"

"It isn't just you. It's called being a human being, boy. In particular, a male human being."

"Yeah."

"How old are you, Jimmy?"

"Twelve. Three weeks ago."

"Uh-huh. Let's talk about something else."

# 12

I patrolled the streets, partly out of duty, partly sheer restlessness. I had a powerful sense of life spinning out of control, flying to pieces. A sense of impending change, one I could not predict, but which filled me with vague dread.

I missed Amanda to a surprising degree. I'd cared more for her than I'd realized. How much of it was simply physical attraction and infatuation and how much was something more, I couldn't say. All I knew was that the thought of her dying in a deliberately caused train derailment overwhelmed and saddened me beyond expression.

I glanced down the street . . . and stopped in my tracks.

I could think of no reason anyone should be inside the Gullytown Church at that hour, on that night of the week. Yet I'd just seen someone slip inside the door. I paused and watched . . . and a dim light became visible through the opaque, rippled, colored glass of the single side window of the little house of worship. Whoever had gone inside had just lighted one or more of the lamps that hung in sconces all along the interior walls.

I headed toward the church. As I neared I realized I might be overreacting to a perfectly innocuous situation. The Gullytown Church kept its doors unlocked around the clock so that those who felt a need to pray or simply be in the comforting enclosure of a churchhouse could do so at any hour. Most likely I'd slip into that church and find either its pastor at prayer, or some visitor seeking solace and a place for meditation.

When I reached the church's door I found it locked. The person inside had locked the door behind him, contrary to the policy posted on the outside of the door: THIS PLACE OF WORSHIP OPEN AT ALL TIMES FOR THOSE WHO SEEK THE SOLACE OF PRAYER.

I rapped on the door. "Open up, please!" I called in.

When no one answered I called again. Then several more times. Half a minute later, the door rattled and moved. It swung open and revealed the last face I would have expected to see.

The man behind the door looked at me closely, nodded, and said, "Hello, Dylan Curry. I thought that sounded like you. What brings you calling this evening?"

The speaker was John Byrd, uncle of Jimmy Walsh.

"Hello, John," I said, actually wondering for a moment if I were speaking to a ghost. But ghosts, I figured, didn't look as solid as the figure before me. And probably didn't have breath that reeked of whiskey. "I'm surprised to see you here. But I'm glad. The general perception in town right now is that you are a dead man, killed when the train derailed."

"Yeah, I figured as much. It's been kind of interesting to have just kind of vanished away. Moving through the world but not having to be part of it anymore. Of course I've had to stay hid. You're the first person I've let see me since the train wreck."

"And I was the last to see you before it."

"That's right. Funny, ain't it. I got up on that train with the notion of jumping off and dying. You talked me out of it, and then dang if we both don't get throwed off. Hey, I'm glad you made it through alive, too. Me, I got thrown off into a gully. It was all filled with brush and grass soft enough to keep me from getting killed. It knocked me dizzy, but nobody who came around after saw me down there. I just stayed put and let everybody get gone before I came out. I figured that I might have some trouble because I'd been riding on top of the train. Might 'rouse suspicions that I was part of the robbery."

"Were you?"

"No, Dylan. I swear."

"I believe you." I paused and surveyed our setting. "What's going on, John? I'm more used to seeing you hanging around saloons this time of night than visiting churches."

"Dylan, I'm glad you've showed up here," he said. "I believe the Lord himself must have sent you. I been praying in here, Dylan. Can you believe such as me has been praying? I been asking God to send me somebody to talk to. I think that must be you, Dylan. I've got some confessing to do. Will you come in here and talk with me?"

"I don't know about that, John. You aren't aiming on clouting me on the head as soon as I step inside, are you?"

"No, Dylan. Not at all. I'd not do that to you. I'd never do that kind of thing."

"Sad thing is, you already do that very thing to your nephew. I've seen Jimmy with bruises bigger than you could paint on with a barn-painter's brush. And you know the worst thing about it? Despite the way you've treated him, Jimmy still grieves because you've been gone and he's thought you are dead. Grieves for *you,* John. I saw the boy this very night, fed him supper. You're not fit to have so fine a nephew. I've been meaning to talk to you about him and how you treat him."

Byrd blubbered, eyes wet. "You're right . . . and I'm worse even than you know, Dylan. I've gone and did the worst thing of my life, and it's about to kill me, Dylan. I swear I don't know what got in me to do it."

"Are we still talking about you beating on Jimmy?"

"No. Something else. Something worse."

"Something so bad that you considered throwing yourself under a train for having done it?"

His voice was soft and cracking. "Yeah. Something that bad."

I took a stab. "John, did you take on a killing job?"

He looked at me as though I'd just read his mind out loud. "How did you know?"

"A lucky guess and a bit of calculation."

"I'm ashamed of myself, Dylan."

"You should be. And the most shameful

part is the fact that it was a woman."

He swiped at his wet face with the heel of his left hand.

I stepped inside and we closed and locked the door behind us. Walking up the single aisle between the rows of simple wood-bench pews, we reached the front of the church and sat down on the front pew.

"You must be a good lawman, Dylan, to have figured out about that killing job," John said.

"I am a good lawman, but this one didn't take a lot of skill. For one thing, it takes something big, generally, for a man to get to the point of being ready to throw himself under a train. Besides, word went out on the pipeline out of St. Louis that there was killing work in Gullytown. It wasn't hard to make the connection."

"Yeah."

"But how could you do it, John? You're no killer. How could you take a man's money to kill his wife?"

John Byrd quit crying all at once and gaped at me.

"Just what do you think I've did, Dylan?"

"Well, John . . . based on seeing Amanda Seabury nearly get shot down by a gunman hidden in a grove of trees just outside town, and based on what she herself has told me,

I think what you've done is that you've taken on the job of killing her under the hire of her former husband back in St. Louis, a man name of Brannigan. That's why you were in St. Louis, right? You went to see the man who'd hired you to kill Amanda Seabury. To close the deal, so to speak."

"You got it wrong, Dylan. I wasn't hired to kill Amanda Seabury. Just the opposite. Hell, I was hired *by* Amanda Seabury!"

My heart sank. "What did you say?"

"Amanda Seabury hired me to kill her husband for her. Or maybe it's her former husband . . . I can't remember what she said, and that part don't matter. He was unfaithful to her. 'Betrayed her' is how she put it. She wanted him to pay for that with his life. She said that she has a vow with herself that no man who ever betrays her will be suffered to live."

"Have you done that killing job, John? Did you kill Brannigan while you were in St. Louis?"

"No. No, didn't get the chance. To tell the truth, I got distracted by all the saloons. Got drunk and never had the opportunity to do the job. But I got close to him. Almost close enough to take a shot at him through his own window. Something stopped me

240

from doing it, though. Then he saw me and run me off with a shotgun . . . and that's when it hit me, just how low I'd sunk. I'd traveled all the way to St. Louis to kill a man for money. God, there ain't no lower than me."

"But you didn't do it. So it's not too late to back out. And besides, it's a dead issue, anyway. Evidence is that Amanda Seabury was on the same train we were, John. Remember what you told me up on the train, about how you weren't the only stowaway?"

"Yeah, I remember."

"Apparently that other stowaway was Amanda Seabury. Did you know at that time that it was her?"

"I didn't know."

"Well, apparently she was hiding in a boxcar. They found the body afterward. I've seen it. Too mangled up to recognize, but all indication is it was Amanda."

He took all this in, brows knitting. "I knowed there was somebody in that box-car . . . I could hear them moving around. You feel right certain it was her?"

"Most likely her, yes, like I told you. It's bad for her, but for you, John, it's a way out. Your employer for the killing job is gone, which means the job is gone, too."

241

"But . . . I already took some money from her. Does that make me guilty?"

"I don't know. I'm no lawyer or judge. You've made no actual attempt to kill Brannigan at this point, right? You didn't actually take a shot at him, right?"

"I took a shot, but not at Brannigan."

"At who, then?"

"At *her*. She paid me to do it. But she didn't want me to hit her. She gave me money and told me to shoot at her and miss, but come close enough to make it look like I was trying to kill her. You were there with her the day I did it, Dylan. That was the plan. She wanted you to see her nearly getting shot."

It made sense all at once. I understood her game. All along the advertised killing job had been *her* job, *her* hiring out of the murder of her betraying former husband. But part of the scheme, to keep me and the local law off her back, was to make it appear that *she* was the target, the intended victim. And what better way to solidify that illusion than having someone actually take a shot at her in the presence of an officer of the law?

That conniving woman had played me like a cheap fiddle! I wondered why I couldn't have figured it out before. Maybe because

John Byrd had done too good a job. That shot he'd fired at her had come too close, actually grazed her. John had made that shot just a little *too* convincing.

It was like the world had started spinning in the other direction all at once. My belief in Amanda's veracity, which had been held in place mostly by a combination of infatuation and a sheer will to believe in her, trembled and collapsed.

"Are you going to arrest me?" John asked.

"I don't know that it's worth the bother, if Amanda Seabury is dead. All you've done so far is take money to shoot at someone and deliberately miss. I don't know that there's even anything illegal about that. Confound it, John, I feel a fool. She's played me and the law for imbeciles. I've danced to her call just as nice as you please, as stupid as a monkey on a grinder's leash."

"She had a way of making men want to do what she wanted, Dylan. She was so damn *pretty*! It was prettiness that made me say yes to what she offered, Dylan. Her prettiness, and the good money she paid."

"Did she tell you much about Brannigan?"

"She said she was married to a man older than she is. A rich fellow. But the rich wasn't enough to make up for the old — that's the

243

way she put it to me. And he ended up being unfaithful to her, anyway. God, he has to be a fool to be unfaithful to a woman as beautiful as that."

"There's beauty that's on the outside, and there's deeper kinds. I don't think Amanda Seabury had much of the deeper kind of beauty, John. The kind inside."

"Reckon not. But damn, she had plenty of the kind on the outside!."

"She did have that." It felt unnatural to speak of her in the past tense.

Talk stopped a while. John Byrd seemed lost in thought.

Finally he spoke again. "You're right about me not being a fit uncle to Jimmy, Dylan. I ain't. And I ought to be horsewhipped for it. He's a good boy, and like you said, he's all I got left of my poor sister, God rest her. It's too bad she didn't have nobody better than me to leave her little boy to when she got sick. Why do good folks like her have to die, Dylan? Why do pieces of rubbish like me go on living, and she dies?"

"I can't answer those kinds of questions, John. But I can tell you again that, if you don't like the man you are, you can change."

"I don't think I can, Dylan. I'm too far gone into the bottle ever to get out of it again. I'm just a lost old sinner, and always will be."

"Well, when I was growing up the preachers always used to say that the only sin that couldn't be forgiven was failing to ask to be forgiven," I suggested.

"It's too late, Dylan. Too late. I agreed to kill a man, and there's nothing worse than that."

"There is. There's actually *doing* the killing, and you haven't done that, John. And the woman who hired you isn't in the picture anymore."

John Byrd stood and paced across the front of the church to where a big wooden crucifix hung on the wall. He stood staring at it, saying nothing.

I began to leave and John turned and called to me. "Dylan."

"What is it, John?"

"I just thought you might want to know what it was that stopped me from shooting Brannigan through his window."

"Tell me."

"I was afraid I would hit her instead of him."

"Her?"

"Yes. Amanda Seabury. She was at the window with him when I saw him."

I was nearly floored. I'd wondered where

Amanda had gone after she left Bellfield Hospital. I would never have guessed she would have gone to the very home of the man she claimed to fear most, the man she had sworn was trying to kill her.

"Did you know before you went to his house that she was there?" I asked.

"No. But I knew how to find the house because she had told me. I figure she must have gone there herself to try to get him to show himself at that window so I could get off a shot at him. But I held fire because she was too close to him, and then he saw me and all I could do was run."

"Did you see her after you ran?"

"No. No. And now you tell me she's dead."

"John, help me think this through. Why would Amanda have stowed away on the train rather than using her ticket?"

"Maybe she was hiding from him. Maybe he figured out she was trying to get him killed, and she had to run from him."

I nodded. John could well have been right. But there was another possibility. Maybe that dead body I'd seen in the coroner's parlor had not been Amanda after all. Maybe she had never gotten on the train at all for the return trip. Maybe she was being held by J.P. Brannigan. Or maybe she was already dead long before the train pulled out.

I left John Byrd in the church alone and returned to the streets to patrol. I'd walked halfway across town when I heard the sound of muffled gunfire. Shots, coming from the northwest side of town, where some of the foulest dives of Gullytown were located.

I checked the loading of my pistols and headed that way on a trot. Merciful God, what a night it was turning out to be!

And it wasn't over yet.

# 13

The sound of shooting had stopped by the time I reached the part of town from which it had come. Almost as an afterthought, I reached into my jacket, pulled out my badge and pinned it on my chest. This corner of town was comprised of crude, unpainted warehouses, stables, a dirt-floored gambling house, a couple of shacks, a "church" that met in an abandoned saloon under the pastoral oversight of a town drunk, three rough houses, one of which housed a brothel Henry Myers had never been able to shut down, plus one operating saloon, worst in town, and a blacksmithy that was seldom open.

I hugged the corner of the warehouse and peered into the narrow street, lighted only by a crude streetlight consisting of a lighted torch on an upright pole. At first I saw no people other than the barely visible outline of a shirtless man peering out of the brothel window, and a handful of other men huddled in the doorway of the rough little saloon. Nothing to tell me exactly from where the shots had come, who had fired them, and whom they had been aimed at.

I opted not to draw my pistol yet, but I did put a hand under the flap of my coat to hold the pistol grip, just in case.

Carefully, I proceeded, moving so quietly that at first I did not draw any obvious attention from those in the saloon doorway. I slid along the front of the warehouse, mostly hidden by shadow, then heard a thumping, heel-on-wood kind of noise the origin of which I could not immediately ascertain. I drew the pistol, but positioned it so that my body hid it from the men across the street.

Reaching the alley, I peeped around the corner into it and heard movement. A voice spoke from the shadows. "Dylan? That you, Dylan?"

It was the voice of Bert Rader, one of my fellow deputies under Marshal Myers. Rader sounded odd, voice tight and strained. I stepped into the alley and raised my pistol, looking for my colleague.

"Bert?"

Bert's bulky figure materialized in the shadows. But he moved differently than usual, walking along with one shoulder brushing the wall, using it for support. And when he got close enough, I knew he was bleeding even though it was too dark to see it. I had ridden with bushwhackers, knew war. Knew the distinctive smell of blood.

"Bert, what happened?"

"I been shot, Dylan. Through the side. Dug a hole through me under the skin, then came out. Made a kind of tunnel through me, but far out enough to the side not to hit anything vital. I'll be all right, I think, but it hurts like a hot poker."

"Where's the gunman?"

"In the warehouse."

Bert shuddered and slumped hard against the wall, and began to slide slowly down. I shoved my pistol back into its hideaway holster and grabbed at my codeputy. Bert's trembling legs seemed to find a little strength and his slow descent halted. With a painful effort he pushed himself back up again.

"You lean against the wall, Bert. I'm going to get somebody to fetch a doctor."

Bert nodded. I left him there and headed out of the alley to the street. The same men were in the door of the saloon across the street. "Hey!" I called to them. "We need a doctor over here! Somebody get one!"

The men rumbled and shifted. None

moved to get a doctor. I drew my pistol and fired it into the sky. No reaction. These men were not easily scared.

But from them a figure emerged, a boy, squeezing out of the saloon and into the street. I looked closely. Yes, it was who I thought it was.

"Hello, Dylan," Jimmy Walsh said. "I thought that was your voice."

"Jimmy, boy, what are you doing hanging around in a saloon? You're too young for such foolishness. I thought you'd gone home."

"I was looking for Uncle John," Jimmy replied, heading across the street to me. "He's alive, Dylan. He's really alive . . . I saw him with my own eyes tonight. He was crossing the street. He got out of sight before I could get to him."

"I saw him too, Jimmy. After you and I headed our separate ways tonight. I saw him over in the Gullytown Church, praying and such."

Jimmy gaped. "Praying?"

"That's right. Would you have ever guessed it? He says he wants to be a better man, and treat you better. But he's got a lot on his mind just now."

Jimmy touched my arm. "Which one is shot?" he asked. "Is it Bert Rader or Leon-

251

ard Spradlin?"

"It's Bert. Jimmy, can you get a doctor for him? Nobody else is going to do it . . . wait. Wait! Did you say Leonard Spradlin?"

"Yes, sir. That's who shot it out with Bert. I saw him with my own eyes . . . and so did Bert, after I pointed him out. Then Spradlin saw that Bert had his eye on him, and Bert had his badge on, right there for him to see, so Spradlin knew Bert was a deputy. He run off, hid in the building yonder behind us, and shot Bert after he went in after him. Bert was brave, going in like that."

"He surely was."

Someone emerged from the alley behind us, and I wheeled and whipped out my pistol, lowering it when I saw it was Bert Rader.

"Bert, you danged fool, you . . . what are you doing walking? You're shot, man . . . sit down on that porch there and let us fetch a doctor to you."

"I'm strong enough to walk, Dylan. I do need the doc, but I can get to him myself."

"Bert, is it true what Jimmy here tells me? That Leonard Spradlin is the one who shot you?"

Bert nodded. "It's true. Couldn't believe it was him, but I saw him clear enough to know it was. So I went to arrest him, him being wanted, and we exchanged shots. He shot me, but I think I hit him, too."

"So Spradlin's wounded, too."

"Yeah. But I don't think I hurt him bad. I think it was a bad shot."

"Spradlin's probably watching right now," Jimmy said, flicking a glance toward the front of the warehouse. "Maybe listening."

I took Jimmy by the shoulder and wheeled him to face me. "Jimmy, I want you to walk with Bert and get him to the doctor. And tell the doc I may have another patient for him soon. I'm talking about Spradlin. Can you do that for me?"

"Yes, sir!"

Bert was pale and seemed in pain.

"Bert, are you sure you can walk?"

"I can make it. I had my arm nearly shot off in the war and walked three miles before I found a field hospital. This is easy compared to that."

"Off with you, then. Stay close to the boy."

"Dylan?"

"Yeah, Bert?"

"He's in the warehouse. He'll kill you, Dylan. Spradlin hates law. He'll kill you."

"He may try. There's a difference between trying and succeeding."

The boy and the wounded deputy walked down the street and around the corner. Just before they rounded it, Jimmy looked back at me and called, "Be careful, Dylan Curry!"

"I will, Jimmy."

I walked back into the alley, pistol in hand, wondering if Leonard Spradlin could see me. There were no windows facing the alley, but the building was old, rough, and built of knothole-punctured lumber, so Leonard might have a relatively good view of the entire alley. It was also possible that Leonard was not in the warehouse at all any longer. There were certainly ways out on several sides of the rambling building, and it seemed likely that Spradlin would have detected or at least suspected the arrival of law enforcement after the noise of the shooting exchange between himself and Bert, then fled the scene out of simple prudence.

I sneaked toward a small rear door through the warehouse wall. I entered quietly, thanking heaven that the door hung on leather hinges and did not squeak.

Once inside, I slipped into a dark corner and squatted there, looking around and letting my eyes adjust to the darkness. The only windows in the big empty building were on the front and west side, opposite my location, and admitted little light. Just enough illumination was available to let me eventually begin to make out shapes and forms in the darkness.

The warehouse was, on its lowest level, simply one huge room with a couple of office rooms sectioned off near the front. But above was a massive loft spreading across almost all the building, though it ended short of the rear wall so that, in my current position, I could look up all the way to the underside of the roof. A little farther into the building and I would have been able only to see the underside of the loft floor.

Where was Leonard? Did he remain in there at all? The longer I looked around, the more I felt I was alone. So I began to relax a little, and even slipped my pistol back into its holster. Rising, I took a step in the direction of the center of the warehouse, moving out into the open.

Glancing up, I froze. Standing on the edge of the loft was a man; he leaned against a support post, looking down in my direction. He was in a dark spot and was almost invisible, but I squinted hard and was sure that really was a human figure I was seeing. The man didn't move at all.

I knew that I was bound to be far more visible to him than he was to me, so I figured there was no point in playing games.

I straightened, looked up directly at the shadowed figure, and said, "Leonard! Leonard Spradlin! Is that you?"

No movement, no reply. Then a faint groan from above, and a slight shift of posture, and the man leaned out and fell, causing me to jump back in alarm. He plunged from the loft and hit hard at bottom. At first I thought he'd died on the way down, but he groaned again and rolled over, onto his back. In the slightly better viewing conditions below the loft I saw how sodden with blood his shift was.

A candle in a holder was attached to a nearby post. I lit it and two others I found, and provided much better light.

"Leonard?" I said. "It's Dylan Curry . . . remember me?"

His eyes fluttered in that birthmarked face of his and managed to stay open a few moments. He looked at me and his head actually nodded a bit. "Curry," he whispered, with effort. "I'm . . . hurt."

"We'll get you to a doctor, Leonard," I said, surprised he'd been able to talk at all. "We'll get you patched up."

"Amanda . . . where is she?"

Amanda? Why was he asking about Amanda when his own life hung so in the balance?

"Have you not heard about Amanda?" I asked. "The indications are she had stowed away in a boxcar of the train you and Kirk derailed. A body was found, badly torn up, that apparently was hers. She's dead."

He closed his eyes and groaned loudly in a way that made me believe it was for more than physical pain.

He was fading. He'd be dead before long unless I could spur him to try to hold on through sheer force of will. So I decided to get him talking as best he was able.

"I've seen you with Amanda in Gullytown," I said. "Remember the day you were in the boardinghouse and ran out because I'd seen you? Amanda tried to say you were someone else besides who you are. Why did she lie about that, Leonard? And what was the nature of your association with her?"

That was a lot of questions for a badly hurt man and I didn't figure he'd try to answer. To my surprise, he opened his eyes fully and managed to hold them that way. He sucked in a breath that obviously hurt, and spoke in a raspy but unexpectedly strong voice. I realized that this was a man with something he had to say in the brief time he had left to say anything . . . something so important to him that he would expend the last of his mortal energy to get it said.

And what he told me in those next several moments before he died was the most surprising information I could have received.

I left Leonard Spradlin's sad corpse lying unattended by any but the rats that filled the warehouse. As I exited out a rear door I could hear their gnawing teeth devouring the bloody shirt he wore. They had descended upon him as soon as I left. It made me shudder. I felt that the right thing would be to go back and scare them off, but what did it matter? He was equally dead, rats or not, and the vermin would only return when I left, anyway.

I headed straight for the office of Dr. Ralph McClune, the only real physician in Gullytown. It was to McClune that Jimmy Walsh had led the wounded Bert Rader. Though McClune normally did not keep official office hours that late, he was usually easy to find in an emergency because his office was at his home. The doctor, a single man with a religious bent, didn't drink or gamble or womanize, so he was not tempted out of home by the saloons and gambling dens and dance halls. He'd been right there and available when Jimmy Walsh had come pounding on his door with the pallid and weak Rader teetering at his side.

I found Henry Myers present as well. Though he'd been off duty that evening, he'd been notified by someone that there had been shooting, and had strapped on his Remington pistol and hit the street. By luck or fate he'd passed the doctor's place at just the time Jimmy Walsh and Rader had come to its door.

Rader was propped up on a bed in a back room of the doctor's office area. Lacking a true hospital, Gullytown had to make do with a little suite of rooms in the doctor's place. At the moment Bert was the only patient. He wasn't hurt badly enough to require being kept there overnight, but the decision had already been made for him to remain. Bert was single, living in a room above an apothecary shop on Stewart Street on the other side of town. The doctor, knowing Bert for the clumsy and careless man he was, feared he would somehow further damage and worsen his wound, stumbling about his place alone, trying to take care of himself. Best just to keep him where he was and make sure the wound got a chance to begin to heal.

"You did a better bit of shooting tonight

than you knew, Bert," I said. "That was a clean shot Spradlin took. He's dead now. Died as I knelt by him. How'd you two come to exchanging shots, anyway?"

"He saw my badge, I think. I didn't do nothing in particular to provoke it except for telling him I knew who he was. I reckon he figured I was going to try to arrest him, and he wasn't having none of it. He drew his pistol and that made me have to draw mine."

"You got in the better shot," I said. "You're still here, and he's gone."

"I can't believe Leonard Spradlin has been killed right in my own town, by one of my own deputies," Marshal Myers said. "Damn! I don't like his breed coming here. Gully-town won't be a haven for them who are on the run from the law. I'll not have it."

"With fighting deputies like Bert here to shoot them down, that ain't likely to happen," I said, and Bert beamed with pride.

"Good work, Bert," the marshal said, shaking the deputy's hand. "You'll go down in law-keeping history as the man who killed Leonard Spradlin."

"Aw, hell!" Bert said, straining for humility. "Spradlin ain't such big stuff. He was just a low-level kind of bad man. Helped out old Kirk and that was about it. On his own he wasn't much."

We spent a few minutes more with Bert, reassuring ourselves that he was indeed not seriously hurt, then took leave of the room and headed out into the street. Jimmy still wanted to find John Byrd, so we went looking. He wasn't at the church any longer, nor in any saloon we looked into. Eventually Jimmy headed for the shack of a home he and his uncle shared, figuring he might find him there. Sober, I hoped. Despite John Byrd's avowed wish for repentance, I didn't trust him to cease beating Jimmy. He'd have to prove himself on that one.

When Jimmy was gone, I roused the local undertaker and sent him after the body of Leonard Spradlin in that warehouse. Whatever the rats had left of him, anyway.

# 14

The spirit of enterprise was alive in central Missouri in those days, and in the momentary absence of a working railroad, an old-fashioned ox-wagon freight company got rolling, hauling goods between St. Louis and Gullytown on wagons of the sort that had fallen into virtual disuse with the advent of the railroad. It would be a short-lived venture, everyone knew, because the Colonel had aleady replaced the ruined but heavily insured railroad cars with new ones pulled in from St. Louis by special train. The Gullytown Line's locomotive, though, had suffered boiler damage in the derailment. The boiler had ruptured in the area where it had been repaired earlier, filling the locomotive with fire. Fortunately, the engineer and fireman had at that time already been thrown clear of the train, so the usual crew fatalities associated with boiler ruptures had been avoided. But it was taking longer to replace the locomotive than it had the damaged railroad cars.

So, along with a wagon freight company, a stagecoach line had also sprung into being, no doubt destined for as early a demise as the freight line would have. The railroad would not be gone for long. Modern times wouldn't allow it.

The Gullytown Mercantile Emporium had a large, covered front porch. Usually it was well stacked with merchandise carried out each morning and moved back inside each night. Among the items were four old rocking chairs that no one ever showed inclination to purchase, but which were immensely popular as a place to rest a few minutes, or even a few hours, and have a smoke and a bit of conversation with whatever other loafers filled the other chairs.

I was in one of those chairs, talking with Mrs. Finch's friend Sugar Kenzie, when the stage rolled in and came to a stop in dust and rumbles. Sugar leaned back in his rocker and sighed.

"I know you are a railroad man, Dylan, but I have to admit, it's pleasing to see the stage running again. There's hardly a more miserable mode of travel, yet there's always something soothing in seeing a coach roll into town, carrying who knows what, and who knows who. Does that make any sense to you, or just sound like an old man's foolishness?"

I shifted in my chair. "I understand entirely, Sugar. I kind of like it, too. People have been riding in coaches for scores of years . . . hell, *centuries* of years. So yeah, it's satisfying to see the old ways come back even if only for a short time."

Sugar shook his head thoughtfully. "Ah me, I guess if it was up to me nothing would ever change, Dylan. I'd just keep life all familiar and comfortable and be happy for it."

"I can understand that, Sugar."

The coach came to a full stop; the driver threw the brake and began climbing down from his perch. The young fellow at shotgun was lighter and quicker and was down, then up the back to begin removing luggage from beneath the protective oilcloth atop the stagecoach. While he did his work, the door opened and passengers began to disembark.

"Now, there, my friend, is some magnificent lip hair," Sugar said, gesturing at a stoutly built fellow who had just climbed out of the coach. And certainly he was right. The man, in his midfifties and quite well dressed, had one of the most flamboyant mustaches I'd ever seen. It flared across his face in coifed, gravity-defying splendor, its ends twisted into waxed and pointed tips.

For reasons I could not start to put a finger on, the arrival of this stranger struck me as significant. I watched him take his luggage — a single, fairly large trunk — and heave it on his shoulder powerfully, oblivious, it seemed, to what must be a significant weight, given the thump the trunk had made when the coachman put it to the ground.

I knew this man. The sense of recognition was too strong for me to put it down as co-incidence. I'd run across this fellow before, somewhere, but danged if I could remember where.

A couple of local boys approached the fellow with the offer of hauling his bags for him to wherever he was going. He rebuffed them rudely and left them disappointed as he stalked away.

I said a quick good-bye to Sugar Kinzie, got out of my rocking chair, and followed the newcomer, keeping a good distance back. That sense of knowing this man heightened. But all the thought I could give it did not reveal any clues.

And here was the oddest thing. The man generated in me not only a feeling of famil-iarity, but also of unrest. Maybe even endangerment. I wasn't glad to see him.

Like most newcomers to town, the mustached stranger headed for the hotel. I watched him enter, held back a few minutes to give him time to register, then wandered into the lobby.

"Hello, Joe," I said to the clerk, looking around the lobby to see that the newcomer was not there.

"Hello, Mr. Curry," said the young clerk. Nice fellow, Joe Scully was. He'd been a source of helpful information to me more than once.

"Joe, I need you to do something for me," I said. "Are you allowed to tell me the name of folks who take rooms here?"

"Well, Mr. Adams tells me I shouldn't," Joe replied. "But you know, sometimes I forget to close up the register. And I can't stop somebody from reading it if it's lying open, can I?"

"Guess not. Show me how it is you forget to do that."

He grinned, reached down, pulled out the heavy register and placed it on the desk. "I generally put it up here like this for guests to sign in," he said. "And then I get to doing something else, like maybe carrying somebody's luggage up the stairs for them.

And when I come back down I forget to close the register."

I nodded and looked down at the pages. The book was open to a prior week. I flipped pages until I reached the current day's date.

"I . . . I think I heard someone call from upstairs," Joe said. He headed out from behind the desk and went up the stairs.

The last name listed on the day's register was that of Jonathan Perry Brannigan. Room 209.

Now I understood why he had seemed familiar when I saw him disembark from the stagecoach. It was that mustache, which Mark Hannibal had described to me when I visited with him in St. Louis.

Closing the register, I put it back behind and under the desk before Joe returned from upstairs.

J.P. Brannigan, right there in Gullytown. And not making any particular effort to hide it. He hadn't even bothered to use a false name at the hotel.

Why had he come? Amanda was not there. My best guess was that he'd managed either to figure out who his would-be assassin John Byrd was, or at least that he had come from Gullytown. Maybe he was there to take some revenge for John's failed attempt to shoot him through the window of his own house.

I went outside onto the street and walked around the hotel, eye on the second-floor windows. I picked out the one I thought went with Room 209. The curtain was closed. Nothing to see from out there.

Someone approached me from behind. Something brushed against my left forearm. I turned to see lanky Mandy Wiles, daughter of the local newspaperman Ralph Wiles. She was no more than twelve years old but was nearly as tall as I was, though no bigger around than a telegraph pole. She was as homely as her troublesome father, for whom she worked as a street vendor of his newspaper.

"Here," she said. "It's the latest edition. Papa said to be sure to give you one if I saw you. It has the story in it of you shooting the outlaw Leonard Spradlin."

"What? I didn't shoot Leonard Spradlin! That was Bert Rader who did that!"

"Oh . . . well. I guess that's wrong, then. All Papa had heard was that it was a local marshal's deputy who did it. He figured it was you. He figured it had to be you. He's always said that Bert Rader is useless as a bull tit when it comes to deputy work. He'll be mighty surprised to hear it was him who killed Spradlin."

"Yeah, and Bert will be mighty surprised to see me getting credit for his work in the local paper. Go back and tell your father I appreciate his efforts to build me up in the public eye, but that I don't really need or want that. Tell him to be more careful about what he writes."

She nodded solemnly and seemed quite sad at my obvious state of displeasure. I'd long had the suspicion that the girl found me an appealing specimen of manhood, something probably bolstered by her father's determination to portray me as often as possible as the reigning hero of central Missouri.

She wandered off and I returned to where Sugar Kenzie and I had been seated when the stagecoach rolled in. There I read the newspaper's sorely inaccurate recounting of the incident that had left Leonard Spradlin dead.

It didn't bother me all that much except for the dejection I knew it would cause Bert to feel. He didn't have a notable reputation as a lawman, and now his one achievement big enough to earn him a lasting place in Western lore was being credited to another.

If I'd bothered to think the matter through

further, I might have felt an additional concern: how would Morgan Kirk react to the news, erroneous though it was, that his longtime partner and ally had been killed by the Guardian? The man had pride and a vengeful spirit.

This was one achievement in law enforcement that I would have been glad to see credited to Bert Rader, not to me. Morgan Kirk's path might cross mine at some point. When that happened I didn't want him having the notion that he owed me any of that vengeance he was so famous for.

I folded up the newspaper and laid it on the ground beside my chair. As I did so I noticed another headline, this one on the obituary page. I picked up the paper again.

The story was datelined Gryner Hill. It described the death, funeral, and burial of a well-known woman of that town: Mrs. Jane Samuels Kirk, who had been ill for more than a year. The obituary noted that she was loved by her community and family, was a faithful member of the Gryner Hill Methodist Church as long as her health permitted, and that, ironically, she was also known for being the mother of a man whose life and values had been notably different from her own: the outlaw Morgan Kirk.

# 15

I took my dinner alone that evening in the Palace Restaurant, seated at the same table where Amanda and I had dined on her first evening in Gullytown. The solitude was pleasant, though I didn't much relax, remaining on the lookout for J.P. Brannigan until my meal was done.

I patrolled throughout the remainder of the evening, keeping an eye on the saloons and such until well after midnight. Weary, I finally headed to the boardinghouse, eager to climb into bed.

On the way, I passed the hotel and noted that Brannigan's window was dark. Asleep, I supposed, unless perhaps he was out drinking or gambling in one of Gullytown's dives. But I'd been in such places all evening and had not seen him.

As I reached the boardinghouse I looked up and noted a dimly lighted window. Somebody still awake and burning a lamp.

And then it hit me: the window was the one in Amanda's old room.

I climbed the stairs to my own room, let myself in, and hung my shoulder holster rig and hat in the wardrobe. I slipped off my boots and put them away as well, wiggling my toes and popping my arches.

Curious about that light in Amanda's room, I walked shoeless out into the corridor. When I reached the closed door of Amanda's old room I saw faint light spilling through the crack under the door. And to my surprise heard a shuffling sound like someone moving inside the room.

I'd assumed that most likely Mrs. Finch had lighted a lamp to clean the room and simply forgotten to put it out when she was done. Maybe not. Maybe Amanda was still alive and had come home.

Surprisingly nervous, I lifted my hand and gently knocked on the door.

Dead silence on the other side of the door. If anyone was in there, that person had frozen still at the sound of my knock. Or maybe the room was empty

I put my face close to the door panel. "Amanda?" I called in softly. "Amanda? Are you in there? It's me . . . Dylan Curry."

I heard quick movement inside the room. The knob rattled, turned. I stepped back

272

slightly as the door opened.

The face of Amanda Seabury, as beautiful as ever, looked out at me. I almost fell backward in shock.

"Dylan!" she said, voice quivering.

"You're alive!" I declared, too excited to appreciate that I could hardly have made a more obvious and unnecessary comment.

Something strange happened just then. Her eyes left my face and looked past me into the darkness of the corridor. Her expression twisted into one of instant terror.

I turned just in time to see the broad face of J.P. Brannigan behind me, moving forward in the shadows. His eyes were piercing, angry.

The pistol in his right hand rose and aimed at my face, but he did not shoot. He turned the gun toward Amanda, who was still frozen in the half-opened doorway, face distorted in fright. Then back to me again . . . but by then I'd broken through the shock of it all and lunged at him.

He was big and strong but not fast or reactive. He fumbled the pistol as I reached him. My hand closed around his wrist and twisted. He howled as his hand went weak and the pistol fell from it, clumping heavily to the floor. I kicked it back into the shadowy end of the hall.

The struggle went my way at first because I was younger and faster, but he was bigger, stronger and meaner. My head slammed against the wall, hard, and suddenly all those past injuries I'd suffered echoed through my skull. I began to fall down.

But as I descended I reached out and grabbed his ankle. He tried to pull away, but that only made him stumble. We struggled clumsily, but he managed to keep his feet, and then to kick at me. The toe of his fancy shoe caught me on the side of the chin and again my head spun dizzily.

Grabbing his ankle again, I pulled back hard. I felt him stumble against the railing of the staircase. He tilted, scrambling, grabbing . . . and suddenly Amanda was there, shoving at him, sending him over the rail.

He turned in the air and hit the stairs with a loud crash, then rolled down.

At the top of the stairs I struggled to my feet and headed down the steps toward the fallen man. He was doing the same, but with difficulty. The fall down the stairs had obviously stunned him. He staggered backward and I heard a terrible crashing-glass noise.

I reached him as he pulled himself upright on the lowest stair-rail column. From the corner of my eye I saw Mrs. Finch's door open. She came out, pulling a robe around herself.

Brannigan had a knife. It slashed toward me, barely missing me. Then I saw it was not a knife but a long, sharp shard of broken glass. When he'd staggered at the base of the stairs he'd bumped and broken the glass in the huge bookcase full of the late George Finch's ancient Bibles.

Amanda came down the stairs, stopping halfway down. Weaponless, there was little she could do. Brannigan, meanwhile, continued to attack me with the shard of glass. He connected with my shoulder, cutting through cloth and then skin. I managed somehow not to scream at the pain.

Mrs. Finch disappeared back into her room. I could only imagine how stunned she must feel at the sight of such nocturnal violence right in her own home.

I wished I hadn't disposed of my pistol so quickly when I'd come in earlier. With it I could have settled the matter right away.

Glass cut flesh again, this time my hand. And this time I couldn't squelch a yell. Blood dripped on the floor and my feet slipped in it. I fell down. The bloodied piece of glass flashed just above my head, barely missing me.

I kicked out at him and hit him in the

knees. He stumbled backward and this time it was him, not me, who slipped in the blood. He fell back hard against the bookcase full of Bibles. The case rocked, tilting. The Bibles shifted back, forward, some of them spilling out. A particularly heavy one hit Brannigan on the back of the head, stunning him.

I got up and moved away from the base of the stairs. Dizziness struck hard and I slumped down in the corner.

I saw Brannigan trying to get up again. He held on to the bookcase, which still rocked unsteadily. Brannigan swore loudly, managed to get to his feet, and then lost his balance again, sliding in the blood that had come from the cut on my hand.

He began to fall and flailed out for a handhold to catch himself. He caught hold of the bookcase, but in the process pulled hard on it. It tilted forward, the weight of the heavy books driving it forward and down. It fell toward Brannigan, knocking him forward. His head slammed sideways against the top of the bottom stair column and then the heavy case smashed his skull, his head crushed between the bookcase and the column top. Blood gushed out his nose, one eye closed and the other bulged outward grotesquely, and then he went limp but did not fall flat because his ruined head was pinched between the case and the stair column, holding him in place.

I heard Amanda whimper. She was still on the stairs, having watched the entire terrible encounter.

I got up, still hurt and bleeding a little, and made my way up to her. She sat down on the stair and began to cry. I sat beside her and slipped my arm around her. She leaned into me and wept like a child.

Mrs. Finch came back out of her chamber and went to the fallen bookcase. Leaning and looking beneath it, she saw the horrible sight of what had been J.P. Brannigan, limp and bloodied and crushed.

She looked up at Amanda and me. "He was a wicked man?"

"He was," I said.

She looked at him one more time, visibly struggling not to become ill. But she exerted herself, stood up straight, then bent down and picked up one of the spilled Bibles.

"I knew he had to be," she said. " 'The word of God crushes the head of the wicked.' " She turned, rushed back into her room, and slammed the door.

# 16

"I know about your mother, Amanda," I told her as we walked quietly along a Gully-town side street three days after the violent death of J.P. Brannigan. "I met her in Bell-field when I came there to fetch you that day. And I know her surname isn't Seabury, it's Kirk."

"Yes," Amanda said. "That's correct."

"I talked to her for a bit that day. But she wouldn't tell me who her husband was. So I'm going to ask you, Amanda. Is it Morgan Kirk?"

She pulled her shawl a little higher on her shoulders against the brisk breeze. "Yes," she said. "It is Morgan Kirk. My father."

"Why did you pretend otherwise?" I said. "Where did the name Seabury come from?"

"I read it in a book. I liked the sound of it and took it for myself."

"But why? Were you ashamed of Kirk's criminal ways?"

278

"No," she said. "It wasn't that. In fact, think of me what you will, but there is much I admire about my father's 'criminal ways,' as you termed it. I admire his defiance of authority and society and his unwillingness to live life on anything but his own terms. And I most of all admire his famous vengefulness, his slogan, 'Betrayal brings death.' And that, by the way, is why I refused to use his name. Because he betrayed me. And my mother."

"What do you mean?"

"He abandoned us. I was so small when he left that I can barely remember him at all. He left my mother to raise me . . . but she was not well. Finally she put me out into an orphanage when she couldn't take care of me anymore. Then her health worsened and eventually she was bedridden. My father placed her in Bellfield and paid for her care. But never visited her, seldom wrote. And neither did I, because at that time I didn't know she even was alive. I'd been separated from her when I was a very small child."

"How did you learn about her recently? Leonard Spradlin?"

"That's a very good guess, Dylan," she said. "It was Spradlin. He told me about her, where she was, what conditition she was in, when he came to find me here in Gullytown."

"It was pointless for you to try to pass him off as a horse dealer," I told her. "I knew who he was the moment I laid eyes on him."

"I know you did. But he had demanded of me that I hide his identity. So I did."

"Why did Spradlin come to see you? How did he know you were here? And what did he want from you?"

"He came to see me because my father sent him. And my father knew I was here because I had telegraphed him. I sent a wire to the Gryner Hill telegraph station for delivery to Morgan Kirk. I told him his little daughter Amanda, whom he hadn't seen since she was small, was alive and grown up and in Gullytown. And that I wanted to see him. And perhaps get his help in dealing with a personal matter."

"Brannigan."

"That's right. I'd heard that my father had of late reportedly taken on some killing jobs similar to the kind I needed done. So I thought, why not let him make up to me for all those years of abandonment by killing my unfaithful husband for me? I'd been advertising the killing job through the St. Louis pipeline, but wasn't happy with the kind of people who had responded. Just dull-witted, nearly amateur criminals, mostly. And I wanted someone who would do the job properly, discreetly, and maybe with a bit of flare. So I decided to find him."

"And that's why you found me," I threw in. "Because you had the idea that I had a connection to Kirk and could lead you to him."

"That's right. I'd read Myerson's story about the Guardian in the *Review,* and remember that I told you Myerson himself told my husband that you had once been part of Kirk's gang. I know now that he was wrong, of course, but I didn't know it at that time. So I decided to find the Guardian, and through the Guardian, to find Morgan Kirk."

"I guess I didn't end up being much help. You found Kirk simply by sending a telegraph."

"Ultimately I owe everything to you, Dylan. If not for you taking care of things when J.P. showed up, he'd still be alive and I'd still be in danger."

"Wait a minute, Amanda. Keep in mind that he isn't the one trying to hire a killer. That was you. You were trying to kill him, not the other way around."

"Oh? You think his purpose in showing up at the boardinghouse was to give me roses and tell me he was sorry for being an unfaithful husband?"

"No. And I'd appreciate being spared the sarcasm. He showed up at the boarding-house because he followed me there."

"Why would he follow *you*?"

"I'm guessing he wanted to find out what had happened to his wife during the derailment. Probably somebody pointed me out as the Guardian and he decided maybe I was the man who could answer his questions."

"He had a pistol, Dylan. Remember?"

"Yes . . . and my guess is that he intended to use it on you or me either one if he felt threatened."

"So he was trying to kill me! See?

"Amanda, at that time he had no way to know that you're alive. I didn't know. You'd vanished in St. Louis and never boarded the train. Not legitimately, anyway. Then a body was found in one of the wrecked boxcars . . . a body that looked like it was probably you. Everyone believed you were dead at that time, so I doubt Brannigan showed up at the boardinghouse anticipating finding you there, alive."

"Believe me, Dylan, he would have killed me. The man was evil and he'd come to hate me. And he was unfaithful. He betrayed me."

"Betrayal. That's the theme of all this, isn't it? If anyone betrays you, he marks himself as unfit to live."

"Precisely so. It's a way of thinking I suppose you could say I inherited from my father."

"I hope you never decide that I've betrayed you in some way, Amanda."

"No, Dylan. You've been the best friend I've had throughout all this. And most of all I appreciate the fact you have not arrested me for soliciting murder."

"By all rights I probably should do so. But it doesn't much matter now, does it! Brannigan is dead anyway."

"But there is one more man who has to die. One more betrayer."

"Morgan Kirk?"

"That's right. There is a price he must pay for having left my mother and me on our own for so many years. For leaving her lying in a hospital bed, slowly dying as the years go by. For never being the father I deserved to have."

"Would you like to go to where your father is, Amanda? Right now?"

She looked puzzled. "You can take me to him?"

"Quicker than you might imagine," I replied.

"Then let's go."

The stone was small and unpolished, just a piece of limestone with a name and death date chiseled crudely onto its face. A pauper's gravestone, provided by the county. Amanda gazed at it, confused, then looked at me with an expression shifting toward anger.

"Is this a joke you are playing, Dylan?" she asked. "If so, I don't see the humor."

"This is no joke, Amanda. This is, at last, the truth."

"But this grave is Leonard Spradlin's. Leonard Spradlin was not my father."

"Amanda, I was presented with a rare opportunity the night that Leonard Spradlin died. I wasn't the deputy who shot him, but I was the one with him in the minutes before he passed. He rallied a little just before the end, and was able to talk. And he had something he wanted to say before he was gone."

"What does this have to do with me?"

"Amanda, Morgan Kirk's slogan may be 'Betrayal brings death,' but there was one man, at least, who betrayed Kirk and was allowed to live. Maybe because Kirk was never sure of the facts."

"What are you saying?"

"Amanda, Morgan Kirk is not your father. You have grown up believing he is, and Kirk himself probably believes he is, but two people have known otherwise all along. One is your mother. The other is Leonard Spradlin. The man who fathered you through a love affair with Ophelia Kirk."

"He told you that?"

"Yes. Had to get it off his chest, and my ears were the only ones available to hear it."

"But why didn't he tell me?"

"I don't know. How did he happen to come seek you out?"

"Because of the wire I sent to Morgan Kirk. I told him his daughter Amanda was in Gullytown and that I wanted to see him. He sent Spradlin to find me, I guess to investigate me a bit. To see if I was the real thing, I suppose."

"You had claimed he was a horse trader and seller. Was that at his insistence?"

"Yes. I suppose when you are known as an outlaw you tend to disguise who you are."

"He told you nothing about being your father."

"Nothing at all. Not even a hint. But he did have a strained, scared manner about

him that I couldn't quite explain. Truth-
fully, I thought it was just because he found
me . . . well, it sounds vain to say it, but
through my life I've found that I have quali-
ties that make men . . . *nervous* sometimes."

"You are a very beautiful woman,
Amanda," I said. "Some men can be over-
come by beauty such as yours. Get tongue-
tied."

"Do *you* think I'm beautiful, Dylan?"

"I do. Perhaps the most beautiful woman
I've ever known."

She smiled at me, leaned over and kissed
me on the cheek. Just a light peck. But it
almost struck me lame.

"I don't seem to make *you* nervous," she
said.

"I don't know about that, Amanda. Truth-
fully, you do make me nervous. And full of
questions. You have ever since I met you
and found out you were determined to meet
Morgan Kirk. As I think I told you before,
meeting a murderous outlaw is not an ambition commonly encountered in pretty young
women."

"And I think I told you before that what
is murder to one may be simple justice to
another."

"If you had met Kirk before learning he
wasn't really your father, what would you

have done?"

"I would have first hired him to get rid of my husband. Then I would have found a way to get rid of him, too. Justice, you see. Settlement for all the years he left me abandoned to an orphan's life, and my mother rotting away in a hospital."

I had nothing to say to that. I stood there questioning my own duties as a lawman. It seemed to me that the young woman beside me was potentially as criminal and dangerous as scores like Morgan Kirk and Leonard Spradlin. I was ready to take my leave of her.

"Dylan, does Morgan Kirk know that he is not my father?" she asked.

"I asked Spradlin that same question, but by that point he had talked about all he was able and was just moments away from his death. He said one word: 'Suspected.' "

"So Kirk suspected that his wife had had a love affair with his own friend and partner, and had given birth to a child outside their marriage."

"That's the best I can intepret it."

"I'm surprised he didn't take vengeance on Spradlin, then. And on my mother."

"Maybe he did take vengeance on your mother. He left her alone and bedridden for years and years. As for Spradlin, maybe he didn't know he was the guilty party. I guess we can't know without asking him."

"Then I still need to find him."

"Don't do it, Amanda. Let it go. Live your life and forget the past. And spend time with the mother who never had the opportunity to raise you."

"I suppose I should," she said. "Maybe I will. But you know what I want to do right now?"

I took a wild stab at it. "A platter of fish at the Palace Restaurant?"

"Exactly," she said.

"Then let's go."

As we made our way toward our destination, I asked one more question. "Amanda, why did you pick such a man as John Byrd to try to get rid of your husband? Could you not wait until you found Morgan Kirk, who would probably be a lot more reliable than John Byrd at getting such a job done?"

"It was just a bad decision, I suppose. He'd heard about the job through the St. Louis pipeline, and he wanted the work so badly . . . I thought that with his motivation, he might manage to actually succeed. And he was a good shot, you have to admit that! He was the one who fired the bullet at me from the trees outside town, the one that tore through my skirt. Did you know that?"

"I did. John told me that himself, in a fit of repentance."

"Repentance, eh? Well, I'll believe that when I see it."

"Don't criticize it, Amanda. You could stand a little repenting yourself. You're luckier than you know that I don't haul you into the jail and lock you up."

"Why don't you?"

I shrugged. "I'm not sure. I think I'm just ready for all this to be over. And there's no one left for you to hurt or kill except Morgan Kirk . . . and if you manage that, it will be the best thing you've ever done for your fellow man."

"Just wait. I'll get him."

"But he wasn't really your father, so he didn't really betray you."

"Ah, but he *thought* he was my father when he let me be sent off as an orphan! So it's all the same. He was, in his own mind, abandoning and betraying his own flesh and blood. So I still owe him for that betrayal. He has to reap the harvest of his own doctrine: Betrayal brings death."

The fish was better than usual. I had two plates of it, Amanda three.

The next day I departed for another run to St. Louis. This time Amanda did not go. We encountered no derailers.

Maybe, just maybe, life was about to take a turn toward the peaceful again. I hoped so. I was more than ready.

# ABOUT THE AUTHOR

**Tobias Cole** is a pseudonym for a well-known author of Western fiction. He lives in Tennessee.